Acclaim For
The Works of
GORE VIDAL!

"Few American writers can display the virtuosity of Gore Vidal."
> —*New Republic*

"Highly literate, stylish, entertaining, and provocative."
> —*Wall Street Journal*

"Superb...a grand entertainment."
> —*Harold Bloom*

"Magnificent."
> —*Gabriel Garcia Marquez*

"Always absorbing."
> —*The New Yorker*

"Extraordinarily intelligent and entertaining."
> —*Newsweek*

"Dazzling...wicked entertainment of a very high order."
> —*New York Times*

"What a fascinating book."
> —*Atlantic Monthly*

"Frank, shocking...extremely sympathetic, penetrating and exhortive."
— *New York Herald Tribune*

"A superb story...Fascinating."
— *John Kenneth Galbraith*

"A prodigiously skilled and clever performance."
— *Times Literary Supplement*

"Richly entertaining."
— *Washington Post*

"An excellent book."
— *Chicago Daily News*

"One of the best novels of its kind."
— *Christopher Isherwood*

"America's most formidable man of letters."
— *Los Angeles Times*

"Delectable...Savory...Vidal is the true heir of Oscar Wilde."
— *Bloomberg News*

"[A] grand, teeming affair."
— *Time*

The little man shook his great head. "I have been to many countries. I've done many things. Now I play piano at Le Couteau Rouge."

"What do you know about a woman named Hélène de Rastignac, a French countess?"

Le Mouche sighed. "Many things. I know, for instance, that she is not French, but Alexandrian, and I know that she is not a countess."

"But she is rich?"

"I shouldn't be surprised."

"Was she a spy in the war?"

"Everyone in Cairo was a spy. It was the thing to be."

"Was she one?"

"I have no idea. She was the mistress, though, of Erich Raedermann, who was, as you may or may not know, the most important Nazi agent in Egypt."

This was news. "What happened to him?"

"He was shot, I believe, while with her at their house. She buried him decently. Germany fell. She did not fall with it."

"I met her through an Englishman named Hastings."

Le Mouche whistled softly. "You move in very fast circles, Mr. Wells."

"Too fast, maybe?"

"Maybe, yes. I should be very—circumspect, if I were you. This is not like any other country in the world. People can disappear in this country more completely than anywhere in the world, with the possible exception of Russia, and leave no trace."

"What are you trying to tell me?"

"Only to take care, Mr. Wells. I should hate to see you come to harm…"

THIEVES
Fall Out

by **Gore Vidal**

WRITING AS CAMERON KAY

A HARD CASE CRIME NOVEL

A HARD CASE CRIME BOOK

(HCC-119)

First Hard Case Crime edition: April 2015

Published by

Titan Books
A division of Titan Publishing Group Ltd
144 Southwark Street
London SE1 0UP

in collaboration with Winterfall LLC

Reprinted by an arrangement with
The Gore Vidal Revocable Trust

Paperback edition ISBN 978-1-78329-249-3
E-book ISBN 978-1- 78329-248-6

Design direction by Max Phillips
www.maxphillips.net

Typeset by Swordsmith Productions

The name "Hard Case Crime" and the Hard Case Crime logo are trademarks of Winterfall LLC. Hard Case Crime books are selected and edited by Charles Ardai.

Printed in the United States of America

Visit us on the web at www.HardCaseCrime.com

THIEVES FALL OUT

Chapter One

His dreams grew confused and ominous. Suddenly his muscles contracted in fear and he awoke, sweat cold on his body.

It took him several moments to bring the room into focus. His head throbbed and an ache behind his eyes made the bright sunlight unbearable.

The room was small. Strips of moldering yellow plaster hung from the lathes. The single window was tall, with broken shutters dangling crazily shut, slicing the light in zebra patterns on the warped floor.

The bed was the only piece of furniture in the room: a verminous mattress over springs. When he looked at it, he got to his feet in disgust, staggering a little. From far away he could hear a high toneless chanting. It was the sound that had awakened him, that he had heard in his dreams: the muezzin calling the Mohammedans to prayer, a strange, unearthly noise.

As he picked up his trousers, which lay crumpled on the floor beside the bed, someone began to pound on the door. Through wide cracks in the door's panels he saw the outline of a woman.

"Come in," he said, pulling on his trousers. Then, seeing that the door was bolted, he opened it for her.

She entered the room scowling, a dark-skinned woman wearing a loose robe. She was good-looking, in a heavy way, with large black eyes as bright and unblinking as a rat's.

"American?" Her voice was deep and guttural.

He nodded, fastening his belt and reaching for his shirt. He could remember nothing, yet he was sure he had never seen her before. Vaguely he recalled having paid for a room.

"Money!" The word exploded in the room and she put out one hand in the universal gesture.

"Now, look here...." He shoved his feet into his shoes awkwardly and stood up, working the heels into place.

A flood of abuse made him dizzy. Her hands opened and shut convulsively as she shouted at him, her black eyes large and brilliant. He edged toward the door. She put herself between him and the door, her hands clutching now at his clothes. He shoved her away. This was a mistake, for she immediately yelled for help. Help came in the form of five women of different age, weight, and beauty, but all sharing the same profession and dressed in similar loose robes, all shouting as they crowded about him on the rickety stairs outside the room.

Alarmed, he tried to make his way through this tiger-smelling group, but firm arms prevented him; hands grabbed at him fiercely. With a sudden lunge he broke free of them, and half running, half falling, got down the stairs to the street.

In an arcade two blocks away he paused, suddenly exhausted, sweating in the heat and slightly nauseated.

The bright Cairo noon dazzled his eyes. Shimmering waves of heat made the modern buildings across the wide street quiver as though they were fashioned of gray rubber. He turned his back on the street and looked down the arcade, where, in the shade, men wearing fezzes and sheetlike robes of plain white or striped cotton sat in doorways selling food and shoes and beads and sandals and Coca-Cola. Veiled women passed them without a look to right or left; idle men lounged against the blunt pillars of the arcade, watching the street, where modern cars from all the countries of the world drove gleaming past. He took a deep breath, inhaling all the strange odors of Cairo: musk and food, urine, drugs, filth, and sandalwood. This sudden wealth of new sensation pleased him and he felt better, though still shaky. He reached in the breast pocket of his sport shirt for cigarettes. They were gone. He had bought a pack only the evening before. It must have been a rough night, he thought, moving toward a booth where a grizzled, bearded villain was selling cigarettes.

It was when he came to pay for the cigarettes that he discovered he had been robbed. All his money and his American Express checks were gone. The double-buttoned back pocket where he kept them had been torn open.

Panic seized him as he gave the package of cigarettes back to the old man, who began to whine threateningly, implying that the value of his wares had been decreased by handling. In a daze he moved off down the arcade and retraced his steps to the pale blue building where he had spent the night. When he pounded on the door and shouted, there was no answer from inside. The windows were shuttered against the day and the inmates were invisible. Only a child with red-rimmed, diseased eyes watched him with interest, as he shook the door's knob desperately.

He was given an audience with someone of almost no importance at the American Consulate.

The someone of no importance was young, disinterested, and disapproving. He sat behind a standard American desk in a small bare office with one window so high that the city could not be seen from it. But the noises could not be shut out, high, raucous, breathy Arab noises and, periodically, the unearthly sound of the faithful being called to prayer.

He started right in to tell the young official his story, but he was interrupted.

"I think we had better start from the beginning," said Mr. Case, for so the discreet sign on his desk declared him, gold letters on black. "May I see your passport?"

The document was handed over. "Your name is Peter Wells?"

"That's right."

"You were born…"

"Salem, Oregon."

"And you are…?"

"Thirty-one years and four months old in my stocking feet." Pete Wells was beginning to dislike the young Mr. Case.

"What are you doing in Egypt?"

"Looking around."

"Looking around for what?" The tone was cold and insulting.

Pete controlled himself. "I came here on a ship—worked my way as far as Alexandria on the freighter Roger Hale. I left the ship in Alexandria and came down to Cairo yesterday."

"Why did you come to Cairo?"

"To look at the Sphinx."

Mr. Case ignored the irony. "No tourists come to Cairo in the summer," he said precisely. "July is one of the hottest months and there is cholera in many sections of the city."

"I didn't come for the cholera."

"What, Mr. Wells, is your occupation?"

"My last job was as deck hand on the Roger Hale. Before that I was in the Army five years. Before that—"

"Then we shall list you as a merchant seaman."

"Except for the fact that I lived in Texas and wildcatted, up to the war."

"Wildcatted?"

"Prospected for oil."

"There is no oil in Egypt."

"Now look here, Mr. Case, I'm an American citizen, a first lieutenant in the U.S. Army Reserves. I came over here to look around. I've been robbed and I'm appealing to the government to do something about it."

"It's not the government's…" but Mr. Case paused, deciding not to go into that routine just yet. He made tiny marks on a piece of paper; then he asked, "How much were you robbed of, and where, and how?"

"Three hundred and fifty dollars in American Express checks, about ten dollars in piasters, and my Social Security card."

"How did you manage to save your passport?"

Pete shrugged. "It was in another pocket, in my shirt. I don't know where I was robbed, but I have a pretty good idea it was the house where I woke up. You see, I think I was doped."

"Doped?"

"The last thing I remember was going into a dive a few blocks from here, about five o'clock yesterday afternoon. French place called Le Couteau Rouge. Next thing I knew, I woke up about an hour ago in a house with some woman I never saw before, Arab woman, asking me for money. Well, I couldn't remember a thing, but I was sure I paid in advance, knowing those places, so I got out fast. Then I found out too late I'd been rolled."

Mr. Case's Puritan face was set in a mask of bleak disgust. "Then you don't recall anything between Le Couteau Rouge and waking up this morning?"

"That's about it."

"What do you propose we do about this?"

"I was just going to ask you the same thing." They looked at each other hostilely across the desk.

"I will report all this to the Consul General and we'll see what we can do about getting the Express checks back. In the meantime…"

"I have no money."

"I assume you have a bank account somewhere. The Consulate could probably help you get a check cashed."

"The money I lost was all I have, anywhere," said Pete.

"Your family…"

"No such thing."

"Perhaps we could get you on an American ship, a deckhand job. I assume you belong to the union."

"I just got here," said Pete reasonably. "Maybe you could get me a job."

"Difficult," said Mr. Case vaguely. "The Consulate doesn't like this sort of thing."

"Neither do I."

"Where are you staying?"

"Hotel Stanley, Eugenie Street. I paid a week in advance yesterday, so I've got a place to stay for a few days, with meals."

"Then consider yourself lucky. I'll present your case to the Consul and we will let you know in a day or two if anything can be done." He pushed back from his desk and looked at his watch impatiently; the interview was over.

"What am I going to do for money?" asked Pete, embarrassed by having to beg.

The official looked at him blankly. "I'm sure I don't know," he said.

"Well, thanks." Pete got to his feet. "You wouldn't happen to have a cigarette, would you?"

"I don't smoke," said Mr. Case; then he added, "Sorry," which made it worse, but Pete Wells was already gone.

❖

The Stanley Hotel was only a half-dozen crooked blocks away, a large nineteenth-century building, dilapidated, very English, with high ceilings to which were attached great lazy fans that made little difference in the damp gray heat.

He nodded to the desk clerk, a stubby Britisher with a cockney accent who had told him about Le Couteau Rouge the night before, contributing to his downfall. Then he went into the dining room, where, fortunately, lunch was being served.

Tall Negroes from the Sudan, wearing fezzes, striped robes, and bloomer-like trousers, served him and the dozen other guests, all English, who sat about at the small tables, listlessly eating, their white linen suits crumpled in the heat.

Pete ate hungrily, despite the oddness of most of the dishes and the army of flies that shared them with him. By the time the bitter chicory-tasting coffee was served, he felt more like himself again, as though he could handle anything. The only problem remaining was what to handle. With no money and no prospect of anything from the Consulate, the possibilities for action were limited. He couldn't buy cigarettes or a drink; he couldn't even get into the Cairo Museum, which required a ticket.

His mind full of schemes, he went upstairs to his room. It was on the first floor, facing a cement court where several seedy palms were growing. He shaved. He took a bath in an ancient tub hidden in a dark closet down the hall. Then he put on his only suit, a clean gabardine, old but in good condition, with all essential buttons still attached.

As he combed his hair in the dusty glass of the bureau, he was fairly pleased with his appearance. He looked solvent. No one, he decided, would have suspected he didn't have a cent in the world. His face was eager, healthy, typically American, with dark blue eyes, a small nose a trifle off center, a good jaw, and sandy hair with a cowlick in front that hung over his forehead, like a thatched roof on an Irish hut. He was almost tall, with lean hips and a deep chest acquired during his days in high school and in the Army, where he had been divisional middleweight boxing champion. An honest, open face, he thought to himself with a grin, concealing a larcenous soul. He was prepared to do almost anything to make a dollar, and in his life he'd done a lot of unusual things to survive.

At the moment, the only answer to his immediate problem seemed to be Shepheard's Hotel, where he'd been told almost anything might happen to somebody with an eye on the main chance. That was the hotel where the biggest operators lived.

It was a long walk to Shepheard's and he took it easy, keeping as much as possible to shadowy arcades, trying not to work up a sweat that would wrinkle his last clean white shirt.

Every step he took was an effort because of the beggars, thieves, and guides who clutched at him, shouting, whining, begging, some in English, some in a crazy mixture of French and Arab and English. He brushed them aside, swore at them, but they would not leave him alone, and finally he was forced to accept them as an unpleasant but inevitable part of the scenery.

Shepheard's was a long building, several stories high, with big shuttered windows and a porch on the street side, where, at numerous tables, foreigners and rich Egyptians sat at the end of the day, watching the street and drinking *apéritifs;* but at this time of day the porch was deserted.

With a show of confidence, he walked up the steps to the main door, glad to be rid at last of the beggars, who now fell into position against the terrace wall, waiting for American and European victims.

The lobby of the hotel was blissfully cool after the heat outside. Negro servants in hotel livery moved silently about the great room, carrying bags, doing errands for the guests. Though it was out of season, there were still quite a few guests here, he saw to his relief. Help would come from them, though he was not sure how.

He sauntered from the main lobby into a vast room with a high domed ceiling, like the interior of a mosque, much decorated, ornate, Turkish in style. It was cool and mysterious with dark alcoves in which people sat doing business: fat stolid Egyptians and lean, red-faced British, exchanging papers, peering at small type, murmuring their deals in low voices.

At the end of the room, to the left, was the famous bar, a wood-paneled room with an oval-shaped bar at which stood a dozen men in white suits, drinking, their feet resting on the shining brass rail.

Pete entered the room. He walked its length uncertainly, as though searching for someone. Then, with a puzzled look, glancing at his wrist as though at a watch (his own had been pawned months ago), he approached the one man who was standing alone and said, "You don't happen to know George Whittaker, do you? He's from the Embassy and I…" He allowed his voice to trail off into a shy mumble.

"Whittaker? No, afraid I don't. Supposed to meet him here?"

Pete nodded. "Of course, I made the date kind of vague. You see, I only got here yesterday from the States and I've had so damned many things to do that…" He said whatever came into his head, covertly watching the other: a large-boned middle-aged Englishman with a lined face, dark from the sun, and a bald shining pink skull. He was dressed expensively in a light tropical suit. Pete had already caught the flash of a heavy gold and sapphire ring.

A second before his story gave out, the anticipated invitation came. "Have a drink, sir. Name's Hastings. What's yours?"

"Oh, well, thanks a lot. I will. Peter Wells. A gin and tonic, please."

"American?"

"That's right. Came to Alexandria on a freighter from New York."

"Long trip. Have any plans?"

Pete shook his head slowly. "No," he said uncertainly, as though there were too many possibilities before him. "Thought I'd look around for a bit."

"Sight-seeing?"

"Sure. Pretty hot, though, for that."

"Hot as blazes. Got the country to yourself this time of

year. Just you and the Gyps, as we used to call them in the war. Crew of pirates, but not half bad when you get to know them. I've been around here twenty years, off and on. Middle East man, I suppose. Gets under your skin. Like that Lawrence chap who used to love playing Arab, dressing up, got so he hated going back to England. I'm the same."

Pete listened attentively, enjoying the gin and tonic; then he fumbled through pockets with a stage frown. "Want a fag?" asked Hastings, producing a gold cigarette case, intricately monogrammed.

"Oh, thanks a lot. Must've left mine at the hotel."

"Where you stopping?"

Pete inhaled deeply, happily. "The Stanley. Not a bad place, not expensive."

"What line you in?"

"Oil mostly, before the war. I made a bit of money in the oilfields, in southwest Texas, but then I was drafted, and by the time I got out my partners didn't have much use for me. So I lit out for these parts." Since he was now telling the truth for the first time, he found it easier to look the other straight in the face, and their eyes met. Hastings lowered his first.

"Why Egypt?"

"Rumors about oil in the desert. Thought there might be something here for me."

"Money all over the place, all over," said Hastings absently, watching a group of American businessmen with loud ties move in a boisterous group from lobby to bar. They all ordered Scotch. Hastings shuddered. "Too heavy for days like this. Stick to gin and live longer—kills all bacteria; doesn't injure liver. Think you might like to make a few fast quid in Egypt?" All this came out at once; it took Pete a moment to separate the bacteria from the quid, from the sudden mention of money.

"Why, sure, now you brought it up, I wouldn't mind at all," said Pete, looking carefully at his glass.

"Lot of money floating about. Some it sticks to a man, if he's got the stuff." Abruptly, Hastings' hand closed on Pete's bicep. His fingers were surprisingly strong. Only by flexing his muscles could Pete avoid a bruise. "Bit of all right," said Hastings admiringly, letting his hand drop casually. To anyone watching he seemed to be telling a funny story that he had punctuated by squeezing the American's arm. He smiled tightly, revealing nicotine-yellow teeth.

"I used to box," said Pete. "In the Army."

"Branch?"

"Infantry. Third Army."

"Rugged boy," said Hastings, ordering another round. Pete wondered what he had in mind. They drank the next round in silence. Finally Hastings spoke: "Let me see your passport, if I may. Just put it on the bar in front of me, discreetly."

Mystified, Pete did as he was told. Hastings flicked the booklet open with one finger, glanced at the photo, picked at it with his nail, felt the texture of the paper, and then, all in a half minute, let the passport close. "Thanks very much," he said.

Pete put the document back in his pocket.

"Like you to meet a friend of mine," said Hastings. "Lady who lives here in the hotel. Might have a chat with her. Get to know her. Then later on we'll have a talk, you and I. How does that sound, eh?"

Just weird, said Pete to himself. "Mighty interesting." he said aloud.

"Good chap," said Hastings. "Fact you haven't a bean won't bother her at all," he added, to Pete's surprise.

"There you are, my dear," said Hastings, and he and Pete rose as a slender, dark-haired woman walked toward them from the main lobby. She was dressed in white, very simply, with a tight-fitting blouse that revealed the sculptural line of her figure. She wore no jewels and her hair was drawn softly back from her face, revealing an oval face with black eyes and scarlet lips. Pete guessed her age at thirty.

She gave her hand briefly to each of them. Her smile was brilliant. "Come, let's sit over here, in the shadows." She spoke with an agreeable French accent; her voice was low and musical, "I always feel like a spy when I sit in this room," she said, as they sat around a circular table in an alcove hidden from the lobby by potted plants.

"American…Peter Wells. This is the Comtesse de Rastignac," mumbled Hastings.

"Mr. Wells is very brave to come here in July," said the Countess.

"Came here to look for oil, too, on his own hook. Much braver."

Pete grinned at the Frenchwoman. "Bravery or ignorance,"

he said. "I just thought I'd come out and try my luck. It's usually pretty fair."

"I can see." She clapped her hands loudly and a servant came and took their order: tea. Pete preferred a drink, but he was growing hungry again and the idea of tea wasn't disagreeable.

"Oh…bit of business. Excuse it, Wells. Did the consignment get routed properly?" Hastings' voice became suddenly low.

She nodded serenely. "Everything has been taken care of." She turned to Pete. "How long have you been here?"

He told her; then Hastings interrupted. "Boxer, too."

The Countess looked startled. "What?"

"Boxer. You know…chap fights with boxing gloves, fighter, pugilist. In the Army."

"Ah, how interesting!" She smiled mockingly. "You must give us a demonstration," she said.

"I didn't bring any gloves," said Pete a little sharply, wondering why Hastings had this obsession about his boxing days.

"We don't use them in Egypt, anyway," said the Countess cryptically.

"Must be off." Hastings stood up abruptly. "Can't wait for tea, my dear. I'll call you in the morning. Meantime, keep in touch, Wells. I'm at the Semiramis Hotel. Call me around noon tomorrow. Might have a drink, have a talk."

"I'd like that, sir," said Pete, standing up. They shook hands; then the Englishman was gone.

"I am fond of Hastings," said the Countess as they watched

the erect military figure move off down the mosquelike room to the main lobby. "He is so British that I sometimes suspect he must be an impostor."

"He's very typical, I guess."

"Very. But then, I have that Cairo habit of thinking if anything seems to be one thing it *must* be another."

"And what do *I* seem to be?" He was surprised at his own boldness.

"You? A tourist."

"Nothing more sinister?"

She smiled. "No, I don't think so." They drank hot tea and Pete ate a small soggy sandwich. "How do *I* seem to you?" she asked playfully, her dark eyes shining.

"Like a spy," he said, grinning, remembering her remark when they first met.

She laughed, not at all taken aback. "Well, I will confess that you're not too far wrong. I *was* a spy, for the Free French during the war. But I'm afraid I did nothing colorful. I was here in Cairo almost all the time, spying on the German spies. You have no idea what a silly time it was. At one moment there were eighty-two known spies registered here at Shepheard's, from every country in the world."

"Why so many?"

"Rommel. He was almost in Egypt. No one could stop him. If Rommel had conquered Egypt, then the war would have been over. Whoever controls Suez wins. Until he was stopped, hundreds, perhaps thousands of agents were at work here, undermining the country, watching each other."

"It must've been dangerous work."

She chuckled. "It was absurd, really. I was not very efficient, but I did go to many wonderful parties. It was an exciting time."

"You're French?"

She nodded. "From Paris. My parents came to Alexandria when I was a child. Egypt used to be French—before my time, of course. I was brought up in Alexandria."

"Your family?"

"All dead." Then, guessing at his next question, she said, "My husband is dead, too, in the war. Killed in the *maquis.*"

They were both silent. Pete wondered what to say next. He still had no idea what was expected of him, if anything.

"Why don't you take me to dinner?" This was sudden. "We could talk and you could see the night life of the city. It is very gay."

"I'd like nothing better," he said slowly, "but you see…"

"Good. Meet me here at eight." She rose. Then she added, "You can come the way you are. We're not formal these days." Before he could say anything about his finances she was gone, her perfume subtle and unique upon the air, like jasmine.

He walked about the streets until eight o'clock, staring at the crowds. He was propositioned a hundred times. Boys tried to sell him their sisters, their aunts, themselves; men offered to arrange erotic exhibitions for him, to sell him dope, stolen jewels, Persian rugs. He got very tired of them, but they were a part of this strange world and he was determined to make the best of it.

At eight, exactly, the Countess appeared in the lobby, wearing an evening gown of black lace with a short full skirt in the latest Paris fashion. At her throat diamonds flamed and around her head she wore a filmy veil of black, glittering with jet. Men turned to look at her admiringly as she crossed the lobby. The British ladies in their shapeless evening gowns glared and turned their backs, the highest tribute.

"I'm not late?" She took his arm automatically, as though they were old friends, or lovers.

"On the dot," he said, awed by her beauty. They went down the steps of the hotel. The porter in livery bowed and opened the door to a black sedan. They got in.

"Is this a cab?"

"No. It's a car I sometimes use." She unrolled the window that separated them from the driver, a dark little man in uniform. She said something to him in Arabic and he nodded. She rolled the window back up again.

"You know," he said, "I haven't got any money."

She laughed with mock surprise. "And I thought you had at least one oil well! What a disappointment!"

"You see…"

"Of course you have no money. That's the whole point, isn't it?"

He nodded. She was not always easy to follow. She seemed continually to be suggesting more than she ever said.

"Besides, we won't have to pay tonight. I will sign, like a businessman."

"But I hate—"

"Come, Peter, don't be one of those…how do you say—moral? One of those moral American men."

"I'll try not to be," he said, smiling, aware that their thighs were touching, that his arm was pushed tight against hers, that neither had moved apart although the car seat was wide. "What's your name?" he asked, trying vainly to think only of business. "Your first name."

"Hélène," she said. "But I have never launched a thousand ships."

"You could, I think," said Pete, feeling the slow tickle of desire. But despite the closeness of their bodies she gave him no lead, and so, talking of everyday, they arrived at Mena House, a hotel on the edge of Cairo, across the Nile from the main city and close to the desert, to the pyramids and the Sphinx. From the rose garden where they dined by candlelight they could see the solemn bulk of the Great Pyramid, silver by moonlight. They were the only guests on the rose terrace.

"This is the most romantic place in the world, this garden," she said.

Pete nodded, too contented to speak.

They talked quietly during dinner. It was the best food Pete had had in some months. They drank champagne. They talked of themselves. No mention was made of Hastings, of money, of the present…except for the moonlight. Finally, when they had finished coffee and she had signed the check, she said, "Now that you have seen the beautiful Cairo, I'll show you the more exciting one."

The exciting Cairo turned out to be a nearby night club

called L'Auberge des Pyramides, an exotic, modern place,
like a New York night club with an imported dance band.
Well-dressed men and women sat at the bar or danced on
the small dance floor, which was as small and inconvenient as
any in Manhattan. They were led immediately to a ringside
table by the *maître d'hôtel*, who knew Hélène and seemed
pleased to welcome her.

She ordered champagne again. The orchestra played Cole
Porter. A beautiful silver blonde danced by with a short fat
man wearing dark glasses. Pete found it hard to remember
where he was, that a few miles away the pyramids stood at
the edge of an ancient desert.

Hélène reminded him, though, that this was still Cairo.
"You see that man?" she said, pointing to the one with the
blonde. "That's Farouk."

Pete stared hard at the King of Egypt. He looked, he
decided, more like a dentist than a king. "I didn't know kings
went night-clubbing," said Pete.

"This one does." Hélène looked thoughtful. "Of course,
he's incognito. No one is supposed to recognize him or talk
to him. But look over there." She nodded at the corner of
the dance floor. A square man in a gray business suit stood,
his eyes on the King. Then Pete saw that in each corner a
man stood, hand in pocket, guarding the King. "Make just
one unexpected move in his direction..."

"How about in the blonde's direction?"

She laughed. "Don't tell me you have the American mania
for bleached hair."

"Bleached or real, it's what goes with it," said Pete. He was beginning to feel the effects of the champagne.

Then they danced. He held her very tight, aware of every part of her as they floated on the music, their bodies close together. But this contentment did not last long; after the third number a man cut in.

Pete was prepared to tell him to go on about his business, but a warning look from Hélène restrained him, and he went back to the table alone, leaving her with the stranger. The two waltzed together formally, the distance of her arms between them. The man was tall, with Arab features, swarthy and aquiline. He looked as though he should have been wearing a turban and robe, but he was impeccably dressed in evening clothes and his wiry gray hair was clipped short in the German fashion.

Hélène frowned as they talked to one another. Suddenly she stopped and turned on her heel, leaving her partner alone on the dance floor. On her way back to the table, Pete noticed that the King, who had been dancing with a bored, stolid air, looked suddenly interested; he said something to the blonde. They both looked at Hélène as she came back to the table.

"You took care of that fast."

She shrugged. "Let's not talk about it. I hate people who bother one at a dance, talking business. I want more wine, Peter."

He filled her glass. "Business?"

"Yes. He's a…a rival of mine." She would say no more; but

whoever the man was he had put her in a bad mood, for
after only one dance she wanted to go home.

In the car, on the way back to Shepheard's, Pete put his
arm around her shoulders and pulled her toward him, pulled
the scarlet mouth against his lips. It was all easy, suddenly,
dreamlike and exciting. But then, sensing his excitement,
she pushed him gently away. "You're ruining my veil," she
said.

"To hell with that," he murmured, conscious of a familiar
pounding in his ears; he held her tightly, and this time she
accepted his embrace passively.

At the hotel they got out and she dismissed the driver.
Then slowly they walked up the steps in the moonlight to the
dim lobby, where only a few drowsy servants leaned against
columns, nodding.

There was a difficult moment, for Pete at least, when they
stood looking at one another, she with an odd expression in
her gleaming eyes and he with a roaring in his ears.

She broke the silence. "You can walk me to my room," she
said lightly. "I'm on the ground floor, right on the garden."
He followed her without a word down the high-ceilinged,
dim hall to the right of the desk. Her room was in a corner,
at the end of the hall. She opened the door with a large brass
key. "Come in," she said, without looking back at him.

He followed her into a large room, Victorian, with a brass
bedstead canopied with mosquito netting. She sat down at
her dressing table and removed the veil, then she turned
and motioned for him to sit in the armchair opposite her.

Puzzled, he sat down. Her mood had abruptly changed. She was now cold and businesslike.

"What is your price?" This came with startling clarity.

"Price? Price for what?" For a moment he wondered if perhaps she thought she would have to pay him for making love to her, but this was too extraordinary.

She came to the point quickly. "For your time, for your intelligence, which I hope is high, for your body, which…" She paused thoughtfully; then: "It should take no longer than a week, and it will be dangerous."

"What will be dangerous?"

"What you must do. The errand Hastings and I have in mind for you."

"I'm afraid I don't have a very clear idea—"

"You won't have, for some time." She smiled. "You will have to go up the Nile. It will be dangerous, but with luck and good sense you will be quite safe. You will be paid half in advance and half when you return at the end of the week."

"Return from where?"

"Luxor. It's several hundred miles to the south."

"Paid how much?"

"That is what I asked. I want to know your price."

Pete grinned, amused by the situation. "I'm afraid I don't have any set fee."

"We'll pay you a hundred pounds sterling now and another hundred when the mission is over."

He multiplied that out quickly in his head, around seven hundred dollars in all.

She noticed his hesitation misjudged it for bargaining, and said, "You will be given some fifty pounds in Egyptian piasters for expenses."

"You twisted my arm."

"I what?"

"Old Army expression. I mean you talked me into it. I'll go."

"I'm glad," she said, relaxing a little. Absently she unfastened the diamond brooch at her throat and placed it on the dressing table. He watched her, full of desire, but there was no sign, no signal that she wanted him, and the thought of the money at stake made him cautious.

"When do I go?" he asked.

"I'm not sure." She ran a comb through her dark hair. She was perfectly casual, as though she were alone or with a familiar friend. "Perhaps tomorrow, perhaps in a few days. It will depend on Hastings."

"You are partners?"

"In a sense."

"Will I be told what I am supposed to do in Luxor?"

"Oh, I think so, but not much more." She laughed. "You must not be too curious, either."

"One question: Just how does this proposition stand in relation to the law?"

"You want to know if what we're doing is illegal?" She sighed. "It is so hard to answer. Some would say yes and some would say no."

"The law is usually pretty clear in most cases." Pete was stubborn.

"Perhaps," said Hélène. "Now I think you'd better go. I shall probably see you tomorrow, after you have your talk with Hastings."

"I hope he'll be clearer than you," said Pete angrily. He had not expected the evening to end this way, but the expression in her dark eyes warned him not to make a move yet. Then, too, he was confident that if he really wanted her he would have her, sooner or later. There was a natural law that operated in these matters, he thought, his eyes on her slender legs, which showed clearly through the black silk as she sat, legs crossed, in front of the dressing table.

"Good night," she said coolly.

"Thanks for the dinner." He managed to sound as casual as she, even though his mouth was dry with desire.

"I enjoyed it," she said softly. Then, remembering herself, she added evenly, "Be sure to mention none of this to anyone. Not that it is illegal." She smiled. "It's just that what we are doing is confidential and Hastings and I have many rivals in Cairo. Some of them are desperate men."

He awoke suddenly.

Through the latticed window the dawn gleamed, pale and gray. In its dim light he saw three figures standing over him. He tried to leap out of bed, to call for help, but they moved too quickly for him. Dazed from sleep, he struggled for one brief moment; then it was all over.

They tied his arms behind his back and slipped what seemed to be a pillowcase over his head.

A harsh voice muttered in his ear, "Make noise, throat cut." The accent was Arab. Beyond that Pete could tell nothing about his visitors. He remained perfectly still on the floor where they had left him.

He could hear them searching the room: rolling up the mattress of the bed, shaking out pillows, opening drawers in the battered bureau. Then, after what seemed an eternity in which no one spoke, he was lifted by strong arms and dropped onto the bed.

A surprisingly soft pair of hands moved over his hard bare chest and arms; then, to his embarrassment, his shorts were pulled off and he was subjected to an examination even more thorough than the Army's. When he struggled, a knife's cold blade was held to his throat. When the investigation was over, the same Arab voice murmured in his ear, "We cut you loose. Make no move until we go. Understand?"

Pete nodded. A knife cut his bonds and he was left sprawled on his belly. He waited until he heard the door click shut; then he jumped to his feet, pulled off the blindfold, ran to the door, and looked out into the hall. It was empty.

He shut the door and turned on the light. His visitors had gone through everything, he saw. Even the soles of his one pair of shoes had been pried loose. He sat down heavily on the bed, wondering what to do next. No use to call the police. They had taken nothing; there'd been nothing for them to take. Yet they had been trying to find out something, had suspected him of hiding something in his room.

Well, they knew he had nothing, he thought grimly, re-arranging the bed. There was nothing they didn't know about him now.

It was not until he was about to get back into bed again that he detected a familiar, subtle odor in the room—a scent of jasmine, like that which Hélène had worn.

Chapter Two

The next morning he was called to the telephone in the hall. It was Hastings, who made a date to meet him for lunch at Shepheard's. Pete dressed and went downstairs, his soles flapping as he walked. He would get a new pair of shoes out of his mysterious employers, he decided, still irritated by what had been done to him during the night.

After coffee, he strolled out into the burning street. He was the only person without a hat, he noticed, and since the direct sun was supposed to addle the brain, he kept to the shaded side of the streets, walking with his hands in his empty pockets.

In spite of the unpleasant events of the previous evening, he was soon in a good mood. Even the sight of the bar where he had lost his money did not disturb him. On an impulse, he went in.

Le Couteau Rouge was a dark, wine-smelling bar, very French, with many decrepit travel posters of France pasted to the walls. At this hour it was deserted except for a pair of tired-looking French women with frizzled blonde hair seated at one of the tables, drinking coffee sadly, and a half-dozen English and French derelicts leaning on the bar, talking among themselves.

The bartender, small and fat and bald with a huge mustache and red cheeks crisscrossed with broken purple veins, nodded when he saw Pete. "You have good night Tuesday?" he asked, waddling over, polishing a glass as he talked.

"No, a bad night. I was robbed."

"Quelle horreur!" said the bartender, rolling his eyes. "How much?"

"Everything I had, every cent."

"But this is terrible!"

"That's what I thought, too. You don't happen to remember who I was with that night, do you? I don't remember anything."

The bartender nodded and placed his finger against his nose craftily. "Absinthe," he said.

"What?"

"Absinthe. You say you want to drink only that, and though I warn you because you seem good boy, you don't listen, so I give you four. Four will make people crazy."

Now it was becoming clear. Pete was a light drinker, and he had assumed that his blackout had been the result of a drugging.

"Your name Peter Wells?"

"That's right. How'd you know?"

"I thought yes. Someone from the Consulate call up and ask about you, about the traveler's checks. I say we never see them but we see you."

"Did you see them?"

"Monsieur!" The little man looked injured.

"Just wondering. You remember who I left here with?"

"I no notice. It is busy night. Ask one of these girls. They are here always, see all things."

Peter went over to their table. Both brightened up considerably; in fairly good English, they invited him to sit down. The bartender brought him coffee, implying tenderly that it was on the house. It was bitter and unpleasant but Pete drank it.

The blonder of the two girls had a faint but unmistakable mustache, which shone dark blue against her heavily powdered skin; she knew more English than the other and she did the talking. "We talk to you ever so much Tuesday," she said, patting his arm. "You promise to visit us sometime. We have charming flat."

Pete allowed he would like to visit the charming flat one day; meanwhile, he wanted to know if they could remember what he had done Tuesday night.

The spokesman frowned thoughtfully. "You come in about five and have beer. We notice you immediately because there are so few American gentlemen here in this hot, hot month. Then, after a while, you ask for the absinthe and drink it. Then you talk to all the girls—very nice, though, not like so many American men, who shout and get sick. Then arrives Le Mouche, who plays at the piano nicely here every night, and you talk to him and after a while you sit down and perhaps go to sleep a little in the corner. No one bothers you. It is very gay. Then Le Mouche comes and sits beside you and you drink more absinthe. Then we meet two gentlemen we have appointment with. By then it is very late. When we go you are still talking to Le Mouche."

"Who is Le Mouche?"

"He plays at piano here very nicely, from Lyon, he says, but really he is from Alexandria. But he likes to lie. Oh, very droll, he is."

"When does he come here?"

"When it grows dark. No definite time. We are not so precise in Cairo." They talked a little more, but they had no further information for Pete. As soon as he could, he excused himself, promising that he would visit them one day soon.

His next stop was the Consulate.

Mr. Case had grown no more mellow since the day before. "We have found no trace of the traveler's checks as yet, but they are bound to turn up. It occurred to me, after you left, that if you could give us the serial numbers we would be able—"

"Don't remember them."

Mr. Case looked as though he was not in the least surprised. "In that case, we'll send a cable to the branch office where you bought them and see what can be done about stopping payment. I'm not hopeful."

"Neither am I. In any case, I bought them in New Orleans, Seamen's Bank."

"I will make a note of that."

"What does the Consul say?"

Mr. Case looked at him coldly. "He is a very busy man. I haven't had time to present the case to him yet. When I do, I will let you know."

"Thank you *very* much, Mr. Case," said Pete, and he left the office, allowing the door to bang after him.

❀

Hastings seemed quite cheerful at lunch. His bald head gleamed in the sunlight that streamed into the restaurant through tall windows overlooking the garden at Shepheard's.

"Have a good night, my boy?"

"Only some of it."

Hastings looked surprised. "Didn't like Hélène? I can hardly believe that. Splendid woman. All Cairo at her feet."

"I was at her feet, too, but it didn't do much good."

"Women are funny," said Hastings, as though communicating wisdom.

"Then, after I went home, some people broke into the room and searched it, and me."

"Damned odd! Try the lobster. Believe it or not, they have a marvelous lobster here. Never dared ask, though, where they get it from."

Pete was growing angry. "I don't see why it was necessary for you people to go messing up my room, ruining a good pair of shoes, and—and so on. She could've found out just as much, and more, on her own."

"Think Hélène was there, too?" Hastings' expression was inscrutable.

"I know she was. I got a look at her before they blindfolded me." This was a lie, but it worked.

Hastings nodded. "We'll get you another pair of shoes. Sorry about that. Had to be done, though. Thorough investigation…must be reliable. Hope you understand. Surprised Hélène was there— *if* she was, of course."

"She was, all right."

"All for the best, believe me. Talked to her this morning and she said you'd do. Gave a fine report." And Hastings chuckled as Pete flushed angrily.

The lunch was served them with great ceremony. When it was over, they talked business. Hastings lighted a cigar, Peter refused the one offered him, taking a cigarette instead.

"Now, Pete, my boy, we will get down to cases. Tonight you will take the wagon-lit to Luxor. You will get there to-morrow. You will be met at the station by a dragoman—that's the local word for guide—named Osman. He will take you to your hotel, take care of all details. You can trust him. Now, after you've been there a day or so, sightseeing—must appear to be a tourist—you will be contacted by a Mr. Said. He will tell you what to do."

"And what is that?"

Hastings blew a wreath of smoke about the neck of the wine bottle. "Wheels within wheels, my boy. Remember one thing, though: Keep looking over your shoulder. There may be trouble. Handle a gun?"

"Pretty well."

"Said will probably give you one. Be careful about using it."

"Just what sort of business are you in, Mr. Hastings?"

The Englishman chuckled. "You might say I'm an export-import man." And that was all the information Pete could get out of him.

As they left the dining room, Hastings took out his wallet and counted out, very slowly, a hundred pounds, which he gave to Pete, along with an envelope. "The envelope contains Egyptian currency, expense money as per agreed."

"Thanks," said Pete, pocketing the money casually.

Hastings said with his cold but genial smile, "We trust you, my boy. Absolute confidence you'll come through."

Pete said he was very touched.

"Drop by for dinner tonight," said Hastings, just before he got into the waiting car out front. "Hélène would like to see you, I'm sure, and I'll have your reservation for you. Train leaves at ten-thirty. Come about eight."

"Yes, sir." A thought occurred to Pete. "You don't happen to know a pianist, do you, name of Le Mouche? Works at a bar."

The look Hastings gave him was as bland and empty as ice. "Friend of yours?"

"No. I think I ran into him my first night here, when I was drinking. Thought he might be connected with some traveler's checks I lost that night at his bar."

"Better take it easy. You can get stuck in a place like that."

"Stuck?"

"With a knife. See you later." And Hastings was driven away.

At five o'clock, wearing new clothes, Pete arrived at Le Couteau Rouge. The fact that Hastings had warned him, in so many words, not to go there was all he needed to spur him on. Besides, he was curious to know more about the piano player.

The bartender greeted him pleasantly. "Everything O.K.?"

Pete said everything was O.K. and ordered beer, Munich beer.

The bar was beginning to fill up. Sailors from various foreign navies crowded about the bar. Tough-looking French girls, usually in pairs, sat at the small marble-topped tables that edged the walls, eying the men shrewdly. Small dapper Frenchmen and burly Arab types wearing European clothes seemed to make up the regular clientele. They sat at tables close to the bar, talking to each other, their hands moving excitedly, their eyes turned occasionally on the newcomers at the bar, sizing them up in much the same way the women did. How much money's he got? How drunk is he? Pete looked about sharply when he took his place at the bar to see if there was anyone he recognized or anyone who seemed to recognize him. Except for curious calculating stares, he aroused no particular interest.

The back of the bar was like a dim cavern with more tables, on each of which stood a bottle containing a stump of candle, unlit. They weren't wasteful in this dive, he thought, his eyes straining through the gloom to see what was at the far end. He finally made out, at the very back of the room, a double door to the left of which was an upright piano. More tables, also empty, filled the space from the piano to the bar where he stood. It was obviously too early for those tables to fill up.

Someone pulled at his coat sleeve. He turned and saw the blonde with the delicate mustache. "Oh, hello," he said, making room for her at the bar. "Want a drink?"

"Pernod," she said with a bright smile that revealed dark irregular teeth; she was not his idea of a good time. "You have a good day today?"

He wondered if these people had a sixth sense about money. They seemed to know if you had it or if you'd lost it or if you were going to get it. Love of money was the one thing they all had in common. It was both business and religion to those who lived below the city's surface.

"A real good day."

"I am glad for you," she said, drinking her Pernod daintily, not letting the fine hairs on her upper lip get moist. "I am Parisian," she said, putting the glass down.

Pete said that he could tell she was, which pleased her. It had not taken him long to figure out that being from Paris was about the grandest thing you could be in Cairo. That most of these people were from Alexandria, or maybe Algiers, made no difference; they all claimed Paris as home and talked nostalgically, if inaccurately, about it. Pete played their game with a straight face.

They talked about Paris in the spring, their conversation a bit like the perfume ads Pete used to like to read in the magazines back home. In the middle of a long story about an evening on the Boule' Miche, Pete, reminded by the name of the man he had come here to see, asked her if Le Mouche had been in that evening.

She nodded. "Yes, he came in just before you did. Oh, but this night in Paris was like no other. Maurice Chevalier and I went driving through Montmartre and—"

"Where is he?"

"Monsieur Chevalier? In Paris. I no see him for many, many years, but he—"

"Le Mouche. Where is he?"

"Oh, him. He is probably in his room. Through there."
She pointed to the double door.

"Excuse me," said Pete.

She looked alarmed. "He does not like people back there.
You stay here. Or perhaps we have drink at this charming
flat I have two streets from here."

"I'll be back," said Pete. He moved carefully through the
mob of sailors. They were growing louder by degrees. The
time of good fellowship was at hand, to be followed by wran-
gling and fighting at two o'clock, with the police giving a
hand. Bars were the same everywhere.

The civilians who sat at the table at the far end of the bar
watched his every move. They looked startled when they
saw him go through the double doors.

In front of him was a hallway, lit by a single dim light
bulb. There was one door on the left, one on the right, and,
at the end of the hall, a half-open door through which Pete
could see an alleyway.

He paused between the shut doors, trying to guess which
he should try first. He gave a start when a voice said, "The
door on the left, Mr. Wells."

Pete opened the door, mystified. There had been no one
in the hall.

Le Mouche was seated in an armchair, an electric hot
plate in front of him. On it a teakettle bubbled. The room
was lit by a lamp with a red shade, which cast a ruddy glow
over the chair and the one table, over the prayer rug that
half concealed a window, and over Le Mouche himself, who
waved Pete to a stool beside him.

"I expected you yesterday, Mr. Wells, I was very disappointed when you did not come." Pete stared fascinatedly, stupidly at the man. Le Mouche was a hunchback with a handsome, large, melancholy head and graying hair. He spoke English with great elegance and no accent.

"I—I was busy," he stammered.

"I quite understand, Mr. Wells. After all, you are new to our city and there is so much to see and do."

"How did you know I was in the hall? I mean, the door was shut and—"

Le Mouche chuckled. "Am I psychic? Yes, I think so. Many people have said I can foretell the future, and perhaps I can. But, alas, there is nothing mysterious about my knowing you were in the hall." He waved a long graceful hand at the wall opposite him. Pete saw that two holes had been bored into it, about four feet above the floor, the eye level of the hunchback. "I keep myself informed of what is going on in the bar. This is not a simple city, Mr. Wells, nor, I fear, is everyone as good as he might be. There are even some rather wicked people who cause no end of trouble. One must be watchful." As he talked, very simply, as though to a child, he poured the tea into two cups; then he handed one to Pete. "It is a mint tea, Mr. Wells. Good for the health. The Arabs are especially fond of it."

"Thank you." Pete swallowed some of the hot mixture. It was good.

"Now I have a special surprise for you. I recall I apologized to you Tuesday night for having none of this. Now I can make it up to you." He opened a flat metal box filled with what seemed to be some sort of dark brown candy or preserve. The hunchback scooped out a bit with a silver teaspoon and placed it beside Pete's cup. Puzzled, Peter looked at the lump. "Come, taste it. There is nothing like it."

"What is it?"

"Hasheesh, Mr. Wells, hasheesh. The forbidden fruit, as it were…but the mainstay of the Arab world. Without it they would all go mad, and I am serious. They are forbidden to drink alcohol, but they *can* eat hasheesh, and they do, while drinking cups of hot tea to increase the sensation."

"What is it like?"

Le Mouche clapped his hands and shut his eyes blissfully. "Like flying, like dreaming, only you are conscious all the time and there is no uncomfortable awakening. And of course, to make love when full of hasheesh is like nothing this world can offer. The sensation lasts for what seems to be an eternity, though actually it is only a second or two in actual time."

Pete grinned. "Perhaps I should have a girl, to get the full effect."

Le Mouche took him seriously. "Certainly. Shall I get you one from the bar? As my guest, of course. You can make love yonder on those prayer rugs in the corner. I am sure the Prophet would not mind."

"Oh, well, thanks a lot, but I've got a dinner date," said Pete, realizing how silly he sounded. He was half tempted to accept the invitation.

"As you please," said Le Mouche, and he himself took

some of the hasheesh and chewed it thoroughly, sipping tea from time to time, a faraway expression in his eyes.

"This won't end me like the absinthe did, will it?"

"Certainly not. I wouldn't let you take too much; you know that. Just a taste, to commune with angels."

Pete ate it carefully. The flavor was like ginger candy, sharp but agreeable. As he chewed the pellet, he drank some of the tea. Almost immediately he began to feel warm and relaxed. It was like alcohol, only there was no distortion.

Le Mouche smiled benignly. "Good?"

"Very good. I've got to keep track of the time, though. Have to be at Shepheard's by eight. Important engagement."

"I'll see that you start out in good time."

"The way you did the other night?" Pete was more sharp than he had intended to be.

"I'm afraid, Mr. Wells, that I was hardly responsible for your condition. You insisted on drinking that poison. You were already quite far gone when we met."

"Ah…" Pete relaxed; the drug made the room seem cheerful. He found that he liked Le Mouche very much. Yet, even so, there were questions to be answered. First: "How did we happen to meet? I'm a little hazy about that."

"I should think so." The hunchback poured himself more tea. "I was playing American songs. I believe I had just started something called 'The Memphis Blues' when you came over and sat down beside me and put your arm around my shoulders and said that that was the one song that always sent you."

Even in his warm hasheesh mood, Pete did not like the

idea of his arm around those sad, malformed shoulders; yet it had probably been that drunken gesture which had endeared him to the hunchback. "I guess I'm a sucker for that kind of blues. I never thought I'd be hearing it in Cairo."

"You'll hear it only when I play," said Le Mouche proudly.

"Where did you learn to play our music?"

"In New Orleans—the only place."

"You're not American, are you?"

The little man shook his great head. "No, but I have been to many countries. I've done many things. Now I play piano at Le Couteau Rouge."

"Do you like it?"

"Oh, yes. I see a great deal of life—through those two holes," and his voice was bitter.

A thought occurred to Pete. To his own surprise, he found himself thinking lucidly despite the drug that ran like an electric current through his veins.

"What do you know about a woman named Hélène de Rastignac, a French countess?"

Le Mouche sighed. "Many things. I know, for instance, that she is not French, but Alexandrian, and I know that she is not a countess."

"But she is rich?"

"I shouldn't be surprised. Yes, she must have a great deal of money now."

"How did she get it?"

"How does any lovely girl make money in the world? She had friends."

"Was she a spy in the war?"

"Everyone in Cairo was a spy. It was the thing to be."

"Was she one?"

"I have no idea. She was the mistress, though, of Erich Raedermann, who was, as you may or may not know, the most important Nazi agent in Egypt."

This was news. "What happened to him?"

"He was shot, I believe, while with her at their house on the Avenue Fuad Premier. She buried him decently. Germany fell. She did not fall with it."

"How does she live now?"

"By her wits is the usual expression."

"I met her through an Englishman named Hastings."

Le Mouche whistled softly. "You move in very fast circles, Mr. Wells."

"Too fast, maybe?"

"Maybe too fast, yes. I should be very—circumspect, if I were you. This is not like any other country in the world. We are ruled by a king who is a little mad and, on top of that, we have a number of corrupt officials who make life very difficult for those who refuse to make life easy for them. People can disappear in this country more completely than anywhere in the world, with the possible exception of Russia, and leave no trace." Something in his voice chilled Pete to the bone. He gulped tea quickly, trying to drown the fumes from the hasheesh, which threatened to engulf him in pleasurable waves. With a strong effort, he kept his eyes in sharp focus.

"What are you trying to tell me?"

"Only to take care, Mr. Wells. I should hate to see you come to harm."

"And you think I might?"

"If you get mixed up with people like Hastings and the woman who calls herself De Rastignac."

"Do you know her real name?"

"I suppose I must have known it once. It's not important."

"What is her business?"

"I have no idea. She is involved in many things, and so is Hastings. I was not aware they were working together. It was inevitable, though. They are two of a kind. Will you have more hasheesh? More tea?"

Pete shook his head. "I think I've had it, thank you."

"If you want one of those girls, I would be only too happy to—"

"I'll take a rain check on that," said Pete. He liked the ease with which basic things were handled in this country. "Oh, by the way, you know I was robbed of every cent I had Tuesday."

Le Mouche nodded. "I believe I heard the bartender say so. I was sorry to hear it. If I can help, perhaps…"

"Oh, no, thanks. I'm O.K. now. I *would* like to find out who the hell took my wallet. You don't happen to remember who I left here with, do you?"

The hunchback shook his head. "I believe you left here alone, though I'm not sure. Unfortunately, the street is full of bandits and procurers. It is possible that whoever took you to the bordello took your money at the same time. It is not uncommon. You are lucky to be alive."

"I guess so." Pete stretched his legs comfortably; they seemed to have no weight, to be resting on air.

"You will find life a little less wicked in Luxor," said Le Mouche, pouring more tea. But they were not able to drink it, for someone knocked on the door and said, *"Êtes-vous prêt, Monsieur Le Mouche? Oui? D'accord."*

"I must play," said the hunchback sadly, and he stood up. He was even smaller than Pete had suspected and his body was grotesquely twisted, as though by a giant's malicious hand.

He walked Pete to the door of the bar, their every step noted by the bright quick eyes of the natives. "Have a good journey, Mr. Wells, and guard yourself closely."

"Thanks for everything," said Pete.

"Come see me when you return," said Le Mouche. Then, with a wave of his hand, he disappeared through the doorway of the cavernous bar, like a crab scuttling out of sight.

It was not until Pete was halfway to the Stanley that he realized he had never mentioned to Le Mouche that he was traveling that night to Luxor.

He picked up his suitcase at the hotel and checked out, leaving word that if the Consulate called he could be reached at the Karnak Inn in Luxor. A taxicab took him to Shepheard's.

He was met by Hastings in the lobby. The Englishman was in an expansive mood. "Look quite shipshape," he said, slapping Pete heartily on the shoulders. "Big improvement, eh? New shoes, by God! Come, let's have a drink while we wait for the lady fair."

They sat in the main lobby, only a potted palm separating them from a group of British ladies discussing bridge. They ordered gin.

"All ready for the big trip?"

"All set."

"You'll like Luxor. Colorful, historic, that sort of thing. Some fine lookers, too. If you go in for them."

Pete said he did, although his score so far in Cairo was unimpressive.

"You'll find our friend Mr. Said a big help in these matters. He can fix you up properly. Anything you want. Arab, French, Italian, what have you—or what have *they*. In stock, that is!" He gave a short rumble of laughter. "My advice is try the Arabs."

"I hope to," said Pete, but he was thinking of Hélène now, of how much he had wanted her the night before. He couldn't understand what had gone wrong. In the car she had been unmistakably interested. Then, for no reason, she had frozen. He decided that she would be his main objective when he got back from Luxor.

He wondered as he drank whether or not it was a good idea to mix liquor with hasheesh. Since he felt no ill effects, he decided it would do no harm. The mood of the drug was beginning to wear off, in any case.

"One thing," said Hastings, turning around in the deep wicker chair and fixing his pale stony eyes on Pete. "Keep away from government people—your government, my government, this government. They're *all* bad for us."

"Then we're operating outside the law?"

"If you want to be technical."

"*I* don't want to be technical. I'm just afraid maybe the police will be."

"All of them can be bought, if nothing gets out of hand. Also, don't mess with politics."

"Politics? That's about the last thing I'm interested in."

"Hope so. See that it is."

Pete was mystified, but he had made up his mind to ask no questions until his employers volunteered answers.

Hélène, cool in white, with a flower in her hair, appeared in the lobby. She was as serene as ever when she joined them in their corner. The sight of her reawakened Pete's desire, and also his anger. He would make her pay for handling him the way she had.

But if she was aware of his outraged masculinity, she did not betray it. She spoke lightly, of gossip. "He has done it again, Hastings," she said, after a greeting that had included them both equally, dispassionately.

"Who is that, my dear?"

"The King. This time it's supposed to be a singer, a pretty German girl. You know the one—she sang at L'Auberge, I think, last season."

"Ah! Anna Something-or-other. Mueller? Yes. Handsome creature. Took a fancy to her myself."

"So has he. I'm told the court is in its usual uproar."

"Don't envy the poor child." Hastings shook his head gloomily. "Not my dish at all, if I were a woman."

"Ambitious girls are a class apart," said Hélène. "But now we're doing the dreary Cairo trick of gossiping about the

King to someone who hasn't the slightest interest in what he or any of the other buffoons in this country do. Forgive us, Peter." For the first time since they had met that evening, she looked him directly in the face, a faint, sardonic smile on her lips.

He blushed, remembering the night before. "I'm very much interested," he lied.

They talked for a while of Farouk, of his family, of the intrigues at court. At first it seemed to Pete to be very exotic and Oriental, but after a time the situation sounded more and more familiar to him. The great doings at the Egyptian court were no different, actually, than those in any other society, whether in Des Moines or Egypt or Salem, Oregon. The only difference was in wealth; these rich Egyptians, Pete had soon learned, were the wealthiest group in the world.

They went into the dining room, where dinner was served them. It was very gala, and Pete, still somewhat confused by the hasheesh, enjoyed this luxury, this comfort. He was, at that moment, quite ready to spend the rest of his life in Egypt. For someone who knew the angles it would be a cinch. Not until coffee came and he had sobered up completely did he realize, uncomfortably, that he didn't have the slightest notion what was going on, at least as far as his two employers and the trip up the Nile were concerned.

After dinner Hastings excused himself for a moment, saying he had some telephone calls to make. When he was gone Pete looked at Hélène coolly. "What was the big idea?"

"Idea?" She was examining her face in a small mirror, to

see if her lipstick had been smudged during dinner. She frowned critically at her reflection. She seemed unaware of him, of the hotel guests who paraded past the alcove where they now sat in the Turkish lobby.

"That little show in my room last night, remember?"

She sighed and put the mirror and compact away. "What show? As I remember, we parted in *my* room."

"We did. Then a couple of hours later you and a pair of Arabs paid me a visit and turned everything inside out, looking for something."

"You think *I* did all this?"

He nodded. "I saw you, before I was blindfolded. On top of that, your perfume's unmistakable."

She laughed. "Trapped by perfume!"

"You admit you were there?"

She looked serious. "You must realize, Peter, we can take no chances. As you may have guessed, we're involved in a hazardous game. It had to be done. We found out all about you from the Consulate, secretly, but there was still a chance you might be an agent. The only way we could be certain was to examine you, off guard."

"I'll say you did."

"How modest you American men are!" she said, an amused expression on her face. "Don't forget that I was once an agent myself and I know all the methods of concealment. Believe me when I say our lives depend upon our caution."

"You could have let somebody else do the job."

"But they might have hurt you…and of course it was a labor of love." The mockery was unmistakable and he had an impulse to strike that smiling, perfect face. But he controlled himself; there would be time for that later.

"That's good to hear," he said.

"Any damage they did, we'll put on your…expense account. Isn't that what Americans call it?"

"Were you satisfied that I'm not an agent?"

"Oh, yes. We had no real suspicions, but as I have said, we take every precaution,"

"How long will I be in Luxor?"

"Not longer than a week. Less, I hope." She added this last softly.

"You mean that?"

"Oh, I almost forgot. I have a present for you. I left it in my room. Wait here a moment, will you? I'll go get it."

"I'll walk you to your room," he said, getting up.

"To protect me?" She laughed, but allowed him to go with her.

While he stood in the center of her room, she rummaged through a jewel box. At last she found what she wanted. She turned and gave it to him, a small blue scarab, highly carved, like a seal.

"It will bring you luck," she said. "It came from the tomb of Queen Tiy, a great queen three thousand years ago."

He handled it carefully, impressed by its antiquity. "Will I need luck?"

"A little, perhaps. It is never out of place."

He put the scarab into his watch pocket. They stood for a moment looking at one another, then he pulled her toward him and their lips met suddenly, harshly. She struggled; then she relaxed, as though surrendering. But when he groped for her, she pulled back with surprising strength and struck his hands away.

"You're a rough girl," he said softly, and he moved toward her, quite ready to love, to kill. It was the same thing now, with this strange woman. But before he could seize her again, the door from the hall opened and a familiar voice said, "Thought I'd find you here. Romantic spot. Moonlight on the garden. City of contrast, as that travel fellow in the films would say. But we are in business, children."

"I was giving Peter a good-luck charm," said Hélène calmly, arranging her hair in the glass.

"Thoughtful, very thoughtful," said Hastings in his genial way, but his eyes were as hard as ever, like bits of pale agate.

"We must remember how young our Peter is," said Hélène playfully as they walked down the hall to the lobby. "Young men are a prey to their passions."

"I never was." Hastings chuckled. Pete said nothing.

"But Peter is unusual," she said gaily, taking his arm, her fingers traveling over the hard muscles.

"Well, he's got to tend to his job. Understand, boy?"

"Yes, sir."

"There'll be time for all that later. Now, everything straight? You'll be met in the morning at the station by Osman. Old fellow, small gray beard, spectacles. He will be your dragoman. At the Karnak Inn you will meet, when he chooses, Mr. Said. You will then do what he tells you."

"How will I know him?"

"Good point." He looked thoughtful.

"I know," said Hélène. "We will let Said know about the scarab I gave Peter. He will mention it when he meets him. He will say something about Queen Tiy and you'll know then that it is really he."

"Clever girl. Should have thought of that myself. Must beware of impostors." They were now on the terrace in front of the hotel. The moon shone silver and full in the sky above the darkened street. Several taxicabs were parked in front of the hotel, their drivers arguing softly together. An old British couple sat rocking nearby.

"This is it, my boy, as the soldiers say. Don't discuss these arrangements with anyone. Keep out of disputes. No entanglements of any kind. Understand?"

Pete said that he did. Hastings shook his hand heartily. "See you in a few days."

Hélène held out her hand formally. "Be careful, Peter," she said.

"I will." He looked at her steadily, at her eyes, which shone luminous and fine by moonlight, inscrutable. He realized that he had no idea what she was thinking or what she felt about him. It was an unpleasant thought.

He said good-by abruptly and walked down the steps to the cab. His employers stood on the terrace, pale in the moonlight, until he drove away.

The railroad station was a dismal place, reminding him of the ones in France, only less crowded and dirtier. The usual beggars and pests were on hand and he fought his way through them grimly.

Arab gentlemen, looking as though they should be perched on camels, moved in a stately file toward the train, a nineteenth-century French specimen with an early-twentieth-century American locomotive.

He was shown to his compartment by a cheerful French porter who was voluble in garbled English.

"Here is. Here is, monsieur," he said, sliding a door back to reveal a compartment with a bunk already made up. He switched on the frosted light overhead and Pete gave him the expected tip. "Sleep good. At your service by to ring the bell." He pointed to a button by the bed and then, with many thanks, disappeared down the car.

Not ready for bed, Pete strolled down the corridor. There were few passengers in this car. Most of the natives traveled in second or third class. The third-class carriage that he had passed on the way to his car had been crowded with them, all shouting and laughing with excitement.

On an impulse, Pete crossed from his car into the next, which to his delight turned out to be a dining car, where whiskey was now being served. A half-dozen Europeans sat about in armchairs. He sat down just as the train began to move.

A Negro wearing a fez asked him in French what he would like to drink. Pete told him, and then sat drinking whiskey and soda as the train moved through the outskirts of Cairo, a strange spectacle by moonlight: thousands of mud hovels, each with the yellow flickering light of a lantern in the window. Dark shapes moved quickly in the shadows; other shapes huddled around tiny fires in front of the huts.

The modern city was now only a blur of electric light in the distance, hidden by this sweep of slums, which were as old as the Bible, unchanged since the days of the Pharaohs.

It was several minutes before Pete was aware that someone was staring at him.

The man was seated across from him, a long-legged, barrel-torsoed Egyptian with dark skin, arched nose, and graying hair. When he saw that Pete was aware of him, he concentrated on the cup of coffee before him.

Pete drank slowly, glancing from time to time at the stranger. The man no longer stared at him, although Pete had the sensation that each time his own gaze moved, the dark man's eyes would again rivet on him.

It was with some relief that Pete heard a cheery English voice beside him say, "First trip upcountry?"

"Yes, first trip." The Englishman was ruddy with blurred features. He was in the cotton business and on his way to Luxor. He chattered amiably about cotton, Luxor, and the Labour government back home. Pete relaxed, not listening, soothed by the other's voice, by the comfortable commonplaces he was saying. He tried not to look at the man opposite, and he tried to recall if he'd ever seen him before. He did look faintly familiar, but then, in these last few days, Pete had seen many similar dark faces.

"Of course you must have the police on your side."

The word "police" brought his attention into focus with a snap. He looked at the Englishman. "Why is that?"

"Corrupt, you know. Not like home. All these foreign places

are the same. You must fix them up. Get a key man and all's well."

"Even if what you're doing is entirely legal?"

The Englishman looked hurt. "Wouldn't consider anything else, sir," he said with dignity.

"I didn't mean *you*, of course," said Pete quickly. "I just meant that it seems funny you must pay off when your business is perfectly legitimate."

"Funny to us, but this is Arab country."

Pete had an idea. "Do you know many of the British in Cairo?"

"Quite a few, yes. I've been coming out for ten years, off and on."

"Know a fellow named Hastings?"

The other nodded, his face becoming serious and alert. "Bad lot," he said succinctly.

"What's his line? I happened to meet him at Shepheard's one evening."

"Smuggler, mostly. Black market, that kind of thing. I'd keep away from him."

"I was just curious," said Pete, and then they discussed the King, the favorite topic in these parts.

Finally, his drink finished, Pete excused himself. He left the car with only the briefest sidelong glance at the curious stranger, who was now engaged in studying the interior of an empty coffee cup.

Back in his compartment, Pete undressed slowly, trying to identify the man in the dining car. It annoyed him, like a word temporarily eluding the tongue. He hung his clothes up on a highly ornamented cast-iron hook. Everything was ornate and old, he thought, sitting down on the bunk to take off his shoes.

Beneath the blanket something moved. He jumped to his feet, heart racing. Where he had been sitting there was a lump about the size of a silver dollar; it moved. He threw back the covers and saw a large ugly insect. Disgusted, he rang for the porter.

"Mineral water?" said the plump face peering into the compartment.

"Mineral water, hell. Get that bug out of here."

The porter's eyes grew round and his face paled in spots, producing an unpleasant mottled effect. Muttering under his breath, he rushed down the corridor, returning a moment later with a dustpan and a brush. With great care he removed the insect from the bunk; then, with the back of the brush, he crushed it in the dustpan.

"Very bad," he said, his normal color returning to his face. He was breathing heavily, though.

"I hope to God you haven't got bedbugs here, too."

But the porter was not listening to him. He continued to shake his head, murmuring, "Very bad, very bad."

Pete, a little irritated, asked him what the insect was.

"Scorpion, monsieur. Never before has there been one found like this, *never* before. You must believe me. It is impossible. I clean. They clean. Everyone guards well the filth. There are *never* scorpions on train."

Pete sat down heavily on the bunk, feeling ill. "They're poisonous?"

"Yes, monsieur. Most painful."

"Can they kill a man?

"Seldom, but he becomes sick, oh, sick like the poor soul in hell."

Pete considered the poor soul in hell for a reverent moment.

"The sickness lasts many days," added the porter morbidly.

"About how many days?" Pete was suddenly interested.

"Ten days, maybe less, maybe more."

"About a week, then?"

"A week, yes. Now I will examine the bed with care." While the porter remade his bunk, Pete considered the scorpion, whose poisonous sting might have laid him up for the entire time he was in Luxor. The coincidence was striking, and sinister. Yet who could have had the opportunity to…

Then he remembered where he had first seen the dark man in the dining car: at L'Auberge des Pyramides. He had waltzed with Hélène; she had called him a business rival.

He wondered then if it was too late for him to turn back.

For a long time that night in his bunk, he lay awake, listening to the clatter of the train's wheels as they sped him into the hot barren wastes of Upper Egypt.

Chapter Three

He got off the train shortly before nine o'clock in the morning, before the sun had begun to scorch the streets of the town. Even so, the glare of morning light was blinding and he blinked in it as he stood uncertainly beside the train, a crowd of natives jostling him, trying to get his suitcase away from him.

Except for these usual pests, he was unnoticed in the crowd. The rich Egyptians, wearing white suits and dark red fezzes, moved easily, naturally through the crowds, accustomed to the noise and confusion. There were no Americans, Pete noticed, no Europeans in sight. Suddenly he felt isolated and strange, cut off from his own kind.

He walked slowly toward the station house, a fairly modern building, like those back home. Inside the station he paused. He was wondering whether or not to strike out on his own when an old man, wearing a turban and steel-rimmed spectacles, approached him, smiling, his broken teeth like an animal's fangs.

"Sir Wells," he said, bowing, reaching for Pete's suitcase. "I am Osman, dragoman, sir."

"I was wondering where you were," said Pete, suddenly relieved, even by the sight of this evil-looking old man.

"We shall take the carriage. Sir Wells, to the Karnak Inn," said Osman, without altering his wide, unpleasant smile.

"Good deal," answered Pete, following him out to the street.

There were several battered old taxicabs of obscure ancestry out front, and a number of horse-drawn, open carriages, to one of which Osman guided Pete. The driver, without even looking around, cracked his whip as soon as they were seated, and off they rode through the crowd of milling natives. In a moment they were out of the yard surrounding the station and moving down the dry dusty street. The dragoman sat very straight beside Pete, no longer smiling, his face dignified.

For a few moments Pete was a tourist, watching the houses flash by as their carriage moved through narrow streets, natives ducking out of its way. The houses were two-story, a little like the houses of Mexico, he thought, although the minarets, the red and white striped towers on the skyline, were like nothing he'd ever seen before.

He turned to Osman and said, "Is it far from here, the hotel?"

"Only several minutes from the town, sir," said the old man. "It is on the river."

"The Nile?"

"Is there another river?" The old man looked surprised.

"Very crowded?"

"The hotel? No, sir. This is not the time of year for tourists. The other hotels are closed. Only this one stays open in summer, for people who must come up here to do the business."

"Like me."

An ugly smile split the brown withered face. "You are tourist, Sir Wells," he said, and he sounded more as if he were giving an order than making a comment on Pete's status.

"Any Americans at the hotel?"

"No Americans."

"All Egyptians?"

"I think yes, Sir Wells, but then I am seldom in Karnak Inn," and he inclined his head obsequiously.

Pete sat back in the carriage and observed the streets as they grew more and more rustic, houses giving way to fields of shacks and palm trees until, at the bend of a road, they were on a bluff overlooking the Nile.

"Dry up in summer," said Osman, waving a professional hand at the river, which wound like a gray-green snake through the eroded valley. Even Pete could tell that it had shrunk, leaving sand bars and islands and rock beaches behind. "Libya," said Osman, pointing to a line of skull-white mountains beyond the river to the west. "And the tombs."

"Tombs?"

"Where the jackal god guards the dead kings," said Osman, a strange expression in his filmy eyes.

Pete nodded, uneasy, his flesh prickling a little. Somehow the old man's words had struck an unexpected chord of fear deep inside him…the tombs, the Valley of the Kings, where the mummies of the great Pharaohs lay buried with all their treasure. He began to recall legends, old newspaper stories…. But then they were at the Karnak Inn, and in the rush of paying for the carriage and registering the mysterious fear was forgotten.

The hotel was a one-story ramshackle building, like a house in New Orleans, with shuttered windows, tall ceilings, many overhead fans, flies, and tile floors. The lobby was comparatively cool and dim. Except for a pair of Negro servants leaning with eyes shut against the farthest wall, the lobby was empty.

Osman clapped his hands; it was the Egyptian way of getting service, and very royal in effect. One of the servants ambled forward and took the suitcase. The manager, a dark youth in a gray suit with chalk stripe and Windsor tie, appeared from an inner office.

"Mr. Wells? Yes? We were expecting you. You missed our car at the station? But I see you are in good hands. So hot… " Pete registered, then asked if there were any messages for him.

"No, sir, nothing. Would you like me to show you your room or would you care to have breakfast now? We have a celebrated dining room." Pete said he would prefer to go to his room. The manager himself led the way down a long corridor in the wing that overlooked the river. Osman followed with the porter. It was quite a procession, thought Pete, trying to concentrate on what the manager was saying.

"You are our first American guest in two months…a rarity in hot weather. We have no Europeans here at all in the hotel, except, of course, myself and Miss Mueller. You perhaps know her? She is a very famous artist." Pete said he was pleased to hear it. "She is here to examine the sights. You see, she works in Cairo during the season and this is her vacation. She is enamored of the tombs and spends a great deal of time on the other side of the river. A strange occupation for a young lady who is an internationally famous artist and the intimate of the highest, but then we must allow for human nature, Mr. Wells," said the manager, ushering him into his bedroom. It was a large comfortable room with a huge bed canopied by mosquito netting. Below the window was a strip of garden, the road, and, beyond that, the river. Downriver, north of the hotel, behind a wall of green foliage, Pete could make out the dusty bulk of a temple.

After assuring the manager that all was well and that he would eat presently, Pete was left alone with Osman in the bedroom. They looked at one another thoughtfully. Pete spoke first: "Where is Said?"

"The gentleman will come to us in good time."

"Soon?"

"I have no idea, Sir Wells. Until then you will see the ruins."

"Are you telling me or asking me?"

The old man gave his mirthless leer. "You are tourist, Sir Wells."

"You may have a point there. No ruins today, though. I'm going to get my bearings first. Understand?"

Osman bowed. "I am at your service."

"Where can I find you if I want you?"

"The manager will see that I attend you, sir. Ask him. But I shall be nearby all the time."

"That's good news," said Pete, and he gestured curtly to

the door, Osman bowed himself out, almost bumping into a
tall figure who hurried by so fast that Pete caught only a
quick glimpse of the man who had sat opposite him on the
train.

The celebrated dining room of the Karnak Inn was not quite
so bad as Pete had suspected; he did not mind cockroaches as
long as they were not on the menu. Paper gummed with glue
hung from the center of each slowly revolving fan, attracting
those few flies that were not already busy with Pete's breakfast.
He brushed them away and ate hungrily. Through French
windows opposite him he could see a rank green garden,
bright with flowers. As he was drinking coffee, a woman
entered. He knew immediately who she was.

Anna Mueller was far more attractive than he had imag-
ined. For some reason her name had made him think of a
fat, red-faced German blonde with her hair tied in braids
about her head; the reality was very different.

She was not tall. Her body was perfectly proportioned,
from the smooth straight neck to the small waist and slender
legs; but it was her face that most attracted him. Her hair
was a natural red-gold, more dark than light, like dull copper.
Her skin was naturally pale and her eyes, beneath straight
dark brows, were a deep vivid blue. Her expression was sad.

She hesitated when she saw him; then she moved toward
the French windows. "Would you like some coffee?" His
own voice sounded suddenly harsh in his ears.

She turned, surprised, one hand on the door leading into

the garden. "No, thank you," she said. Her voice was deep, the German accent faint. And then she was gone.

Pete cursed himself for a fool. The first impression was always important, and he had sounded like a high-school boy cruising a Main Street girl. And it mattered, he realized suddenly; it mattered very much the impression he made upon her. Bewildered by his own discovery, he finished breakfast. Then, after lighting a cigarette and counting to twenty to quiet the familiar buzzing in his ears, he got up and walked out into the garden.

He was not sure whether or not she was surprised to see him. Her face was serene. She was seated on a bench beneath an arbor of what looked to Pete like camellias.

"May I sit down?"

"If you like." Her tone was neutral. She moved over to make room for him.

"My name is Wells, Peter Wells."

"You are American?" She turned half around and looked at him frankly.

"That's right. You?"

"I have no country," she said in a matter-of-fact voice, completely without the usual dramatics he had grown accustomed to in Egypt whenever nationality was discussed.

"You are German?"

She nodded. "Düsseldorf, once," she said. "How did you know? My accent?"

"The manager told me the internationally famous artist Anna Mueller was staying in the hotel. You fit the description."

She laughed, suddenly, her face becoming, magically, like a little girl's. "International, yes," she said finally. "Artist, no. Famous, no. Anna Mueller, yes, I am she."

"You sing in a night club?"

"How did you know?"

"I heard about you in Cairo."

She frowned and looked away. "I am so notorious?"

"I didn't say that."

"But that's what you mean, isn't it?" There was a sharp edge to her voice that startled him.

"I don't know what you're talking about. I've only been in this country a week or so."

"I'm sorry. I didn't mean to say that. Forgive me." She was genuinely sorry, he could see, and he forgave her. He talked to her a little about himself, telling her the story of wanting to see the ruins, not mentioning his actual business or his Cairo connections. When he asked her why she was in Luxor, she said, "To think."

"In this heat?"

She smiled. "It doesn't stop the thinking, does it?"

"A little, maybe. Why didn't you go somewhere cool?"

"There is no such place in this country."

"And you have to stay here?"

"I have to stay here." She plucked a flower absently and twirled it between her fingers.

"Have you been a singer long?"

She shook her head. "I am not even a singer now. But they pay me money for some reason. They seem to think the noise I make is worth money, and I take it, of course, I am very poor."

"No family?"

"There is never any family," she said dryly.

"Meaning?"

"That I am displaced. I am the child of Nazis, both dead. No brothers living, no sisters ever born. That is my family history." All this without bitterness.

"You're very young," said Pete.

"I am twenty-one, but I feel as if I have lived through the end of the world, through Armageddon, as we say."

"How did you come here, to Egypt?"

"I went where I could. This was fairly easy. Once I got here, I found work in a night club, and now…"

"You are rich and famous."

"And now I have enough to keep me…independent." Pete understood only too well what she meant by this; he didn't like to think of all the things this girl must have been forced to do to live. It was a cruel business.

"Do you intend to live here all your life? In this country?"

She shrugged. "I have no plans. I have no idea. At the moment I am too pleased to be living at all, and on vacation."

"In the heat."

"I like it." And sitting there beneath the thick greenery, the light filtered green-yellow by leaves, he found that the heat was not unbearable. But then, at that moment, Pete would have found the equator wonderful.

"Will you show me the country around here?"

"If you like." Her voice was impersonal; there was no suggestion of coquetry in her manner. She was direct and uncomplicated, or so she seemed.

"You're here alone?"

"I like being alone." Then, politely: "But I don't mind your company."

"I don't mind yours, either." They smiled at one another. Then Pete asked her if she would like to take a walk now and she said that she would, that she'd show him the temple close to the river, the one he had seen from the window of his bedroom.

As they walked along, chatting to one another, Pete wondered whether or not it was merely his own loneliness that made her seem somehow wonderful, different from any other woman he had known, more exciting in her youthful way than the older, more glittering Hélène. Then, too, he felt protective about this slim blonde girl, and hopeful, very hopeful. He watched her out of the corners of his eyes as they strolled along the palm-shaded road in front of the hotel, the Nile to their right, at the foot of a rocky bluff. She lacked self-consciousness, seemed never to be aware of herself, only of him, of what she was saying to him.

"You should see the tombs tomorrow," she said. "Or soon, anyway, because each day the heat gets worse across the river. It is all desert where the kings are buried, no shade of any kind."

"Will you come with me?"

"You'll need a real guide."

"I have one—old fellow named Osman. He'll chaperon us."

"Yes, I'll go, if you want me to. Here is the temple."

It was a cube-shaped building with squat columns of brown stone and no roof. Inside, between cracks in the stone-paved floor, flowers grew. There were no houses nearby; only a grove of acacia trees separated it from the road. There was a full sweeping view of the river and the mountains beyond that. The temple was deserted.

They walked in silence through the main part, looking at the carvings on the wall, the rows of hieroglyphs. Then, on the other side, through the portico, they found a courtyard with what looked like smaller chapels built around it, to one of which she led him, a shadowy little room with no windows, only a door.

"To think how old it is!"

"How old?" asked Pete, turning to look down at her, at the lovely face pale in the shadows, the eyes shining as she looked not at him but at the tall statue of some god with the head of a hawk.

"Nearly four thousand years, Peter," she said softly. She had said his name at last. It was like magic, like an incantation. He slipped his arm around her and slowly, carefully pulled her to him. Their lips met; he breathed the warm scent of her young body, of her hair, which brushed his face as lightly as the wind. Then, as naturally, they were separate again.

There was a long silence at the feet of the hawk-headed god. At last Anna said, "Why did you do that?"

"Because I wanted to. Because I thought you wanted me to."

"Is it so easy?" and she touched her lips with the back of her hand, as though to feel the impression of his mouth with her fingertips.

"I think so…unless I was wrong."

"Do American men always kiss women when they meet them?"

"I don't know what they do, only what I do."

"Do you do it often? Like this?"

"Very often," he said, telling the truth. "But never like this, Anna."

"You don't know me." And she turned away from him and pretended to examine the carvings on the wall. A man wearing the double crown of Egypt was riding in a chariot, followed by a row of captives, grotesque little figures, all in chains.

"Does it make so much difference?" He studied her straight back. The long hair gleamed in the dim room.

"It would…if you knew." Her voice was even.

"That you have had lovers?" He was moving boldly now, driven on not only by his desire, but by something else, by a power he had never suspected himself of possessing: a need not just for a woman, but for this woman.

"Worse." The word was like a small explosion of bitterness.

"I don't care."

"But perhaps I do." She turned and faced him, her dark blue eyes sad. "We won't talk like this again, will we?" Then, before he could say anything, she pointed to the train of

captives some long-dead artist had etched on the wall with
a skillful hand. "Look at those poor creatures! Prisoners
of war."

"More like freaks," said Pete, wondering if he should
pursue her further or not. He decided to wait, for a time.
"Like a sideshow back home. There's even a hunchback,
like—" For some reason he paused.

She looked up at him quickly, her eyes wide. "You know
Le Mouche?" Her voice was tense.

"Yes, I know him."

"It must be nearly noon," she said, moving toward the
door of the stone chamber. "We should get back to the hotel
before the sun is too hot."

And, try as he might, he could not regain that intimacy
with her that had begun in the ruined temple.

At the hotel they parted in the lobby. When he suggested
a later meeting, she was vague. Puzzled, angry at himself for
having made a wrong move somewhere along the line, he
went to his room.

The revolver was very large, of a foreign make with which he
was not familiar. The way it was pointed at him, however,
was unmistakable, and he put up his hands immediately.

"Don't bother," said the dark man. "This is not a criminal
visit." He was seated at the plain dressing table by the window.
A Tauchnitz edition of an English novel lay open beside him
on the table. He had obviously been reading it.

"I think this is *my* room," said Pete, putting down his
arms and walking over to the bed as casually as he could. He

sat down on the edge of the bed and, with a hand made
steady by an effort of will, lit a cigarette.

"I'm perfectly sure it is," said the other agreeably. Despite
his swarthy Arabic features, he spoke English with a clipped
British accent.

"Make yourself at home," said Pete.

"I've spent a pleasant morning reading while you were
with Fräulein Mueller."

"How did you know that?"

"How does one know anything? I have two eyes."

"Isn't that swell!" Pete mocked him, anger rising in spite
of the ugly revolver. "I've got a pair, too. They were open on
the train when I saw you in the dining car and they were
open in Cairo when you danced with Hélène at that night
club."

The man nodded. "Very good. Very good indeed. You are
not as stupid as you look."

"If you'd like to put that gun down, Junior, I'll show you
who's the stupid one." Pete's upper lip was growing dangerously tight. His muscles twitched. A store of rage had been
accumulating in him ever since he'd come to Cairo. He was
not afraid of the revolver; the other wouldn't dare shoot him
in his own room. He wasn't afraid of the man's body, either,
tall and thickset as it was.

His antagonist only chuckled at his anger. "I have no intention of fighting with you on such a hot day. Where did
you go with that girl?"

"None of your damned business."

"I am from the police, Mr. Wells."

"And I'm from Mars."

"Here are my authorizations." He tossed a passport-like document at Pete. In three languages it announced that the bearer was a police inspector named Mohammed Ali. There was even a photograph. Pete gave the papers back.

"I can put you in jail, Mr. Wells, whenever I choose."

"I'm an American citizen."

"It won't make the slightest bit of difference. Your consulate would never hear another word about you. Our prisons are very uncomfortable, quite barbaric, if I say so myself. You would never be heard from again."

"What do you want?"

Mohammed Ali put his revolver away and teetered his chair back. "At present, nothing, Mr. Wells—or very little. I would like to know what you and Fräulein Mueller talked about this morning, and where you went."

"We went to the temple up the road. What we talked about couldn't've interested you less."

The policeman nodded sympathetically. "She is very attractive, of course. Many people have found her so. I am certain that if you liked, she would be only too happy to accommodate you as she has all the others."

Pete got to his feet slowly, moved two paces forward, and then, with the quick left hook that made him the champion of his division, sent the other man reeling. Mohammed Ali fell to the floor with a crash. Pete stood over him, mechanically massaging the knuckles of his left hand.

"You hit very hard," said the policeman, pulling himself to his feet, one hand held to his jaw. His eyes were suddenly swollen with pain and his face was dark red.

"If you make another crack about Anna I'll do it again," said Pete in a low voice, his body tingling with rage, with this sudden release.

"You don't seem to realize, Mr. Wells, that I can kill you."

"I'm waiting," said Pete, and deliberately he turned his back on the other and retrieved his cigarette, which had fallen, lighted, to the floor; but there was no shot, no attack.

"You're a brave man," said Mohammed Ali, when Pete again faced him. "I should hate to see you killed, because there are so few in the world. I am sincere about that, believe me."

"Thanks."

The policeman straightened his collar. Pete saw, with satisfaction, a livid welt on the man's cheek. "But I am not going to kill you yet, Mr. Wells, as much as I should like to. We will take care of that later on."

"Any particular reason? Or do you just like the idea of shooting American tourists?"

Mohammed Ali sat down again on the chair at the table. "Ah, Mr. Wells, if one were to shoot all the American tourists one would like to shoot, the Nile would be red with blood. No, my reasons for shortening your life have to do with your real mission in these parts You are not here to look at the temples."

"Tell me more." Pete was beginning to relax. He was sure

that sooner or later he would have to pay for his flare-up, but meanwhile he felt wonderful, like a man again. For a few minutes, at least, he enjoyed the sensation of being in charge of his own destiny.

"I must tell you right off that I am on the best of terms with the lady who sent you here."

"Sent me?"

The policeman sighed. "I am doing you the courtesy of being fairly honest with you; at least don't try to deny facts that arc known to me. I know that she sent you here. I know why you are here and what you must do."

"What is that?" Pete was curious to know.

"There is no point in discussing it. I take the view that the Countess's dealings are outside my province, at least in these matters. She and I long ago reached an understanding. I will not interfere. But others may."

"That's real interesting," said Pete, undoing his shirt; he had begun to sweat and the cloth was sticking to his back. He peeled the shirt off and tossed it on the bed, aware that the other was sizing him up like a boxer, gauging power, looking for a soft spot. "Excuse me," he said mockingly. He swung his feet up on the bed and stretched out, still keeping his body poised for action, prepared to spring like a wire coil at any unexpected move on the other's part.

But Mohammed Ali was not contemplating violence, for the moment. "Hélène chose well," he said.

"Those are kind words."

The policeman's eyes narrowed. "You are strong and you

are certainly courageous, but you are a fool, Mr. Wells. You are deliberately antagonizing an official of the police in a country where the police have wide, extremely wide powers."

"You've got a point," said Pete. "But I figure that you're playing a game yourself. You're fairly anxious to use me—for a while, at least. When I get the picture, I'll act differently." He said this coolly, realizing all too well the phoniness of his bluff. But it worked.

"Very realistic, very realistic, Mr. Wells." The policeman nodded approvingly. "It will be an honor to know you. Then let me put the case to you directly. I should like to know when you are planning to go back to Cairo. I will know, in any case, but I should be happier if I could have your co-operation. Second, I strongly advise you not to become involved with Fräulein Mueller."

"Any particular reason?"

"She is involved with someone else. I can't tell you more. If you are not careful, you will offend that someone, and then Allah help you."

"Did he send you to me?" asked Pete innocently, knowing perfectly well who "he" was, but pretending ignorance.

"Certainly not. I pass this information on to you only in the spirit of friendship."

To which Pete said, "Ah."

"I may say that I do more than pass the word along. I must warn you not to see her. If you disregard my warning, then I will be forced to deal severely with you, and I should hate to do that."

"I'm going to do as I please," said Pete pleasantly. "If you interfere in what is none of the police's business, I'll get in touch with a good friend of mine at the American Consulate and he'll make trouble for *you*."

"Meaning Mr. Case?"

Pete was startled, but he betrayed no surprise. "I was thinking of someone else," he said. "I happen to know Case slightly."

"He has not, alas, been able to find your traveler's checks for you."

"What are you up to?" Pete was abrupt.

The policeman fondled his wounded jaw thoughtfully. "I am up to many things. I am here on His Majesty's business, for one thing; even in a casual country like Egypt, officials of the police do not roam about the country on private affairs."

"You intend to interfere with me and the Countess? With my trip here?"

Mohammed Ali shook his head. "Far from it. I may even prove to be co-operative. *You* must be helpful, though. I should like to talk with you after you have seen the distinguished Said Pasha. That, for now, is my only request."

"Sounds O.K. to me," said Pete, pretending innocence.

"In fact," said Mohammed Ali, "I may be of some use to the project." He got to his feet. Pete tensed, ready to defend himself, but the policeman only slipped the book he'd been reading into his pocket, clicked his heels in mock salute, and said, "I must now attend to more official business. Remember, though, what I said about Fräulein Mueller. She is a marked woman in Egypt." And on that curious note, he left the room, closing the door softly behind him.

*

Pete slept uneasily through the hot languorous afternoon. He was awakened, as the rose light of evening streamed into the room, by the ringing of the telephone beside his bed, a venerable brass antique, large and unwieldy.

The connection was bad, but even through the static he recognized Hélène's voice immediately.

"I wondered if you had got there all right," she said, after the usual greetings.

"No trouble getting here," he said.

"Have you seen Said yet?"

"No sign of him."

"But Osman met you all right at the station?"

"He did. I also met another friend of yours, a police inspector named Mohammed Ali."

He could hear a sharp intake of breath at the other end of the wire. "What did he say?"

"He wanted to know when I was supposed to see Said. Wants to talk with me about some deal after I've talked to him."

"Be careful, Peter." The voice was unmistakably urgent.

"I sort of gathered you and he were friends."

"Nothing of the kind. He is treacherous! He promised he wouldn't go to Luxor. Hastings made an arrangement with him, paid him a fee with the understanding that he would not meddle in this transaction."

"He didn't stay bought?"

"No." There was a pause. Then: "I was afraid this might happen. Guard yourself well. You will need a weapon. Said

will supply you. Under no circumstances deal with Mohammed Ali. He's already been taken care of. If he becomes
troublesome…"

"Yes?"

"Do what you can to protect yourself, and our project. It
may be dangerous, especially the trip back to Cairo."

"I'll look after myself."

"I hope so, Peter," and the voice became soft and feminine. "I know you'll be successful. All it will take is a little
courage. You have that, I know. Then we can get to know
one another, if you care to."

"I may take you up on that," said Pete, trying to conceal
his amusement at this obvious tactic. He wanted her still,
but in a different way since he had met Anna; a colder, more
violent way. The first tenderness had gone and only a pure
impersonal desire for that mysterious body remained. It was
a point of honor now, he thought, as he listened to her exotic
voice over the long-distance telephone.

After hanging up, he lay for a few minutes on the bed,
watching the pink light turn to red in the sky outside his
window. A warm breeze stirred the fronds of a palm tree
beneath his window, a peaceful rustling noise. A car back-
fired far away. In the hotel he could hear faintly the sounds
of supper being made ready. For some reason he felt strong
and confident, even though he still had no clear idea of
what lay ahead, of what Said would have him do, of what
Mohammed Ali might do to stop him. It was Anna, he
decided, warm in the memory of her that morning in the
temple. She had given him a center.

He dressed carefully, then, and went downstairs.

The dining room was fairly crowded with Egyptians wearing European suits. They sat eating quietly beneath the bright electric lights that shone harshly, unshaded upon the tables.

Pete was stared at as he entered. He was the only Occidental in the room, except for Anna, who sat alone in a corner of the dining room. Pete walked straight to her table as though by previous plan. Eyes watched him, black, impassive eyes. She did not look up, pretending to examine the plate in front of her.

"May I sit down?"

"If you must," she said, her voice so soft that it was almost a whisper. Her eyes avoided his as he sat opposite her.

"Are you angry with me?"

She looked up then, her dark blue eyes troubled. "No, no. I'm not angry. Why should I be?"

"Because...of what happened at the temple."

"No." A waiter brought them their first course, a sleazy fish full of bones. Pete ordered wine.

When the waiter had gone and attention in the room was no longer focused on their table, Anna said, "I was only sad, Peter, that was all. It is much too complicated a situation. It would be hard to explain it even if I were free to do so, which I am not." She smiled suddenly. "But at least I can—" She stopped abruptly, the smile growing fixed as she watched someone over Pete's shoulder. She spoke quickly, "I am in Room Twenty-seven. If you can, come there tonight, after midnight. Make sure no one sees you."

"Good evening, Fräulein Mueller, Mr. Wells." Mohammed

Ali beamed, as though they were all old friends. He looked more rugged, Pete thought, in his tight-fitting inspector's uniform. "May I?" he asked and sat down, uninvited.

"What brings you here, Inspector?" asked Anna politely.

"Breakers of the law, Fräulein."

"Which laws this time?"

"Smugglers, traitors. The country is full of criminals." He chuckled. "But I'm sure that doesn't interest two foreigners on a visit to our famous ruins."

"We like to hear all the news," said Pete. "You must be full of it."

Anna looked surprised. "Do you know each other?"

It was the Inspector who spoke first, quickly: "We are Cairo acquaintances, Fräulein." Inadvertently his hand traveled to his cheek, where the bruise received that afternoon was only partly hidden by talcum powder.

"We had a talk this afternoon," added Pete, aware of the quick glance Anna gave him, uncertain, questioning.

"Mr. Wells is very much interested in our country," said the Inspector smoothly, deboning his fish with a surgeon's hand. "We discussed politics."

"Politics?" Anna's face was expressionless, but Pete could see that she was nervous.

"Yes. I explained the country to him quite well, I think. He had no idea how democratic it was, how well beloved our King is."

Pete was mystified. Anna was on edge, her face pale. "Are you really so interested in Egypt?" she asked, turning to him, a question in her eyes.

But the Inspector spoke before Pete could admit to confusion. "Certainly he is. Mr. Wells is a student in government. In Mexico he—"

"None of your business, Inspector, what I did in Mexico, or what you think I did."

"Why, Mr. Wells! I thought the Fräulein would be interested."

"I'm the only one who'd be interested in hearing what you have to say, but we can talk about it somewhere else, some other time."

"If you care to hide your light, as it were, I'm certainly not one to offend one who was considered a past master of—"

"Watch it!" Pete's face was set and menacing; he leaned across the table, as though ready to strike.

The Inspector shrugged good-humoredly. "As you say, Mr. Wells. But we were talking politics, not your past distinctions." Pete glanced quickly at Anna. Now she was the one confused; she looked from one to the other, a puzzled expression on her face. The Inspector pretended to notice nothing. As he ate, he talked.

"Although our government is a strong one and devoted to the cause of the people, it has enemies, like any other government. Jewish nationalists, for instance, would like to overthrow our king because of the troubles in Palestine, because we are sending an army into that country to settle its problems in a businesslike way."

"The way you've handled your own problems here?" asked Pete.

"In exactly the same efficient way," and the Inspector

managed to keep a straight face. "But there are other ene-mies. Some people would like to set up a republic, others a dictatorship."

"Not everyone is happy, then?" Pete wondered why the Inspector was talking politics; why, stranger still, Anna should appear so upset.

"There are always malcontents, but we are fortunate in that we have an information service that is probably the best in this part of the world. There is nothing we do not know about." He belched softly as he pushed the plate of fish-bones away.

"It still seems like a good country for a racket," said Pete, unimpressed.

"*Some* rackets," said the Inspector, putting his hand over his glass as the waiter came by with red wine. "In public I am a good Moslem," he said with a sigh. "No wine." Pete drank, however, and so did Anna, mechanically, her eyes vague and her manner distracted.

Mohammed Ali continued to lecture them on the current political situation in Egypt, to Pete's boredom and Anna's ill-concealed alarm. Fortunately, before coffee, the policeman was called away by a whispered message from the manager.

"Excuse me, my friends," he said, bowing low in the Oriental manner. "Duty beckons. Meanwhile, Mr. Wells, bear in mind my words of advice."

"Advice?" Anna looked at Pete, puzzled.

"Oh, sure. Came to me this afternoon with a whole lot of junk, warnings mostly."

"About me?"

"Why do you say that?" Pete looked at her curiously.

She looked down at her plate. "He's right," she said, her voice so soft he could hardly hear it.

"Right about what? I don't know what you're talking about."

The blue eyes were turned on him suddenly, like lights in the sea. "He told you not to have anything to do with me, and he's right. You mustn't see me. You mustn't even talk to me. If—if I weren't so selfish, I would have told you that myself."

"Anna." At the sound of her name she paused. "I don't care what you've done. Do you understand? None of that matters to me."

She smiled gently. "I'm afraid it isn't so much what I've done as what I must do that matters."

"What do you mean?"

"Oh, Peter!" It was almost a sob, but she was a good actress and her face did not give her away to the other guests in the dining room.

"Let's leave the country, now. We can take the night train to Alexandria and get a boat to Naples." He was startled to hear himself say this. It had come out unexpectedly.

She shook her head. "You are sweet, but I couldn't leave now, even if I wanted to. They wouldn't permit it."

"They?"

"Don't ask me any more. For your own sake, please." Then she left him, walking quickly between the tables to the lobby beyond.

Pete finished his coffee, wondering what to do next. He was getting in deeper and deeper, not only with Anna, but

with the whole strange life of this country. His reason told
him that he would be wise to take her advice, and Mohammed
Ali's, to keep his nose clean, not to meddle in their affairs.
But it was too late for that. He wanted her, and not in the
usual way. The body was only a part of it; more important
was the woman, the frightened girl with dark blue eyes and a
soft voice. He could help her; he was sure of that. As for the
Inspector, he was fairly sure he could manage him. It was
unlikely that the policeman would use the law against him.
Without the law, Pete was confident he could handle the
other. He'd been up against tougher ones, smarter ones, and
he had usually had the better of it. He clenched his fist,
thinking of Mohammed Ali.

He spent the time between the end of dinner and midnight
in the lobby drinking Scotch and talking to the manager.

Pete had no trouble getting the subject around to Anna.
The manager had already noted the fact that they had met.

"You like her, yes? A woman of real beauty."

Pete nodded. "She's certainly that. Even the Inspector
seems to like her."

"Mohammed Ali? Yes, he is interested in her, but not that
way. He does not like women." And the manager winked.
This was a new twist, thought Pete, a new complication. He
had heard before that the Arabs tended to like men more
than women; a custom of the country, springing, no doubt,
from the old tradition of keeping women veiled and apart,
unavailable. He recalled uneasily the way the Inspector had
stared at him that afternoon.

The manager babbled on. "No, it is not his interest in the

Fräulein's beauty that causes him to attend her so much. It is because of her friend in Cairo."

"You mean he's been sent here to guard her?"

The manager nodded importantly. "They say he is very jealous. No one knows why she came up here alone, but since she has decided to visit Luxor out of season, we are all honored, of course. Though it's inconvenient having an inspector of the police staying in one's hotel."

"You mean there are all kinds of deals going on in this hotel?"

The manager giggled. "I have no idea, Mr. Wells. I *do* know, though, that the police have a regrettable habit of wanting to be included in ventures that don't concern them."

"Illegal ventures?"

"Ah, Mr. Wells, the line between the law and crime is more vague in Egypt than in your own noble country."

"I bet," said Peter Wells, grinning, remembering some traffic he had got mixed up in at Juarez, Mexico, on the Texas border.

At one minute after midnight, he gave a phony yawn, stretched, and said, "Guess I better be off. Want to be up early tomorrow."

"To visit the tombs, Mr. Wells?"

"The tombs," said Pete, and he walked down the long corridor, his heart beating rapidly, a tightness in his stomach. He paused before Room 27 and looked about him. There was no one in the hall. Quietly he turned the handle of the door. It was unlocked. He opened it.

The room was dark. He was aware of a warm feminine odor. He stepped inside, shutting the door noiselessly behind him. He stood for a moment, back to the door, blinking his eyes until they grew accustomed to the moonlight that poured into the room. Then he saw her seated by the window.

She rose to meet him. They stood silently in the moonlight, looking at one another. Then, still without a word, he took her in his arms, and it was as if a sudden storm passed over them and into them, carrying them to the bed and gathering momentum till finally it exploded in a flash of lightning, leaving them shaken and content. And Pete knew that it had never been like this before.

It was a long time before either spoke. She was the one who finally broke the warm silence.

"It is wrong," and her voice sounded far away.

He kissed her gently on the lips. "It's never wrong," he whispered, holding her as though she were a child. "It's just right."

"I shouldn't let you, Pete, I shouldn't."

"Let me love you?"

"I can't love anybody."

"I don't believe you." He sat up in bed and lit a cigarette.

"I don't mean I can't love you, Peter. If only that were so, I'd be happy; if only I could feel this was like the others."

"Others?" He knew of course that she had had lovers, but somehow he had never quite visualized them. "Many others?"

"Yes."

"You're just making it up."

"If only I were, my love." And that phrase spoken in her soft accent made him tender. "No, Peter, there are many others…against my will, until now. There was nothing I could do, nothing. It was either them or dying, and I was weak and wanted to live. You don't know what it's like to have no money, no home in a ruined country after a war."

"It's over now."

"Yes," she said, "it's over now."

"Let's leave together. As soon as I see a man on some business here, I'll have money, enough to get us out of Egypt, to Europe, maybe even home, to the States. We'll be married."

"Married!" She said the word as though she had no idea what it meant. "You would marry *me*? Someone who… *Ach, Gott!*" and she began to sob. Pete held her close until the sobbing was over, the pain soothed.

"Are you so afraid of him?"

"Him? Who do you mean, Peter?"

"The King. I…I heard gossip. Everyone said you were—"

She laughed, a little bitterly. "No, that is not quite right. I've only seen him a few times. That's all, I promise you. He likes to have pretty girls around him. I suppose, in time, he would have…"

"Is that why you came here? To get away from him?"

"Partly, yes. But don't ask me any more, please. I can't tell you. I *mustn't* tell you. Believe me when I say it is impossible. No, I mean, There is no hope."

"I don't believe it. I want you, Anna."

She gave a long, shuddering sigh. "Then wait, my love. In a

week's time, perhaps. But don't talk about the future. Promise me that."

"I'll try not to."

"And no questions about the past."

He laughed. "There's not much left."

"There's too much left," she said. "I don't want to love you."

"But you do."

"Oh, yes, yes." She turned to him, and all was forgotten but the present. The moon filled the room with pale light. In the hills across the river, a jackal laughed.

Chapter Four

The morning was bright and almost cool. Despite the long night, he was up at eight, feeling wonderfully well. After a cold shower, he went downstairs to breakfast. On his way he knocked softly on Anna's door, but there was no answer. Assuming she was asleep, he went on to the dining room.

After breakfast, he strolled into the lobby, where the manager greeted him brightly. "Beautiful morning! Quite cool for a change. Perfect for traveling, as I told Miss Mueller."

"Is she up?" Pete was startled.

"Up and gone." The manager fussed with a bunch of cards behind the desk.

"Where did she go?"

"I believe she said she was taking the early train to Aswân, just for a day or two."

"Did she leave any message for me?"

The manager shook his head, his hands busy with the cards. "I'm sure she will be back quite soon, though. She left most of her clothes here. Remarkably attractive, isn't she?" and the manager smiled knowingly at him.

"Where is Aswân?"

"South of here, several hundred miles. It's on the river."

"Is there anything there? I mean, is there any reason why she should want to go so suddenly?" He was betraying more

interest than he had intended. The manager was undoubtedly the town gossip, and anything Pete told him would
probably be passed on to Mohammed Ali. Even so, he could
not be casual.

"I'm afraid she didn't tell me. It did seem peculiar, I must
say. Aswân is most dismal."

Pete wanted to ask him the quickest way of getting upriver, but he did not dare. He made some neutral remarks
about the day and then aimlessly wandered out the front
door of the hotel.

His dragoman was waiting for him, the hideous leer
already in place.

"Good morning, Sir Wells! Today is the day we go see
temples at Karnak."

Pete told him what he could do with the temples at Karnak.
Sight-seeing was the last thing he wanted to do. All that
interested him now was finding Anna.

His guide was not easily snubbed. He ignored Pete's remarks. "I have the good news, Sir Wells. Said will see you
this day at Karnak. We meet together in great hall."

"You on the level?" Pete, for no good reason, was suspicious.

"He will be there," said Osman, bowing his head humbly,
getting the meaning of Pete's tone if not the phrase.

"How long does it take to go to Aswân by train?"

"To Aswân, Sir Wells? But you are not going there."

"It's none of your business, Buster, where I go. Get it?"

But the old man did not get it; he only bowed again, a

little deeper. "The train already has gone, Sir Wells. There is only one to the south, early in the morning."

"What about a bus?"

The old man shook his head, not understanding.

"Can I rent a car?"

"It will cost you thousands of piasters," said Osman contentedly, and that ended any hope of his being able to get to Aswân that day. He wondered if he should call the hotel there, to find out what had happened. It was strange, her going so abruptly, without telling him, especially after last night. Thinking of last night, he grew serene.

Osman had hired a carriage and they drove through the streets of Luxor in much the same way they had driven the day before from the station to the hotel. At the far end of the town, Osman pulled a sort of awning over their heads to protect them from the sun. They followed a river road for nearly a mile until, behind a grove of acacias, they saw the massive temples of Karnak: several acres of tall, brown ruins, approached by an avenue of sphinxes.

The carriage stopped at a huge stone gate, and Pete and Osman got out and walked through the gate and into the temple enclosure. Even in his present mood, obsessed with memories of Anna, Pete was impressed.

The temple was very quiet. It was like the one he had gone to see with Anna, only a dozen times as large: a series of buildings of different sizes contained within one wall, roofless, with columned chapels and halls.

Pete followed the dragoman through a series of anterooms

to a great hall full of columns, a forest of masonry that had once been painted bright colors; now only faded smears decorated the dusty stone.

In one corner of the great hall, Said awaited them. He was a small, slight man, neatly dressed in white, wearing dark glasses and a white Panama hat. His face was swarthy and his features sharp, and his hair was beginning to gray.

He smiled when he saw Pete and a gold tooth flashed in the sun. "Mr. Wells, this *is* a pleasure!" They shook hands. Osman backed away from them, his own smile wider and more repellent than ever.

When he was gone, lost among the maze of columns, Said asked to see the scarab Hélène had given Pete. He examined it perfunctorily and then returned it. "Hélène is always so dramatic," he said comfortably. He spoke English well. "Let us take a turn around the hall. Beautiful, is it not?"

Pete said he thought it was very interesting and he listened for several minutes while the other showed him carvings on the wall, explained to him a little about the history of this temple.

Then, in front of a bas-relief of a man in a chariot at war, Said stopped suddenly and said, "History—that is the point."

"Point to what?"

"To everything, to your being here. You have perhaps wondered why Hélène and Hastings wanted you to come to me."

"I never gave it a thought," said Pete heavily. "I just like the heat."

"Very humorous," said the Egyptian, and he laughed shortly.

Pete wished he could see his eyes, but the dark glasses were impenetrable.

"You are here to help us get something out of Egypt. There is a law that you may or may not know: Antiquities, old relics, treasures found in Egypt cannot be removed from the country."

"And you've got something you want to get out?"

"Precisely."

"What is it?"

Said clapped his hands excitedly. "A treasure! Perhaps the most valuable single piece ever found in this country. It is the necklace of Queen Tiy, whose scarab you have in your pocket."

"How did you come by it?"

"That is a long story, Mr. Wells. Let me say, though, there is blood already on the necklace, and a curse." It was strange, thought Pete, to hear a modern man make such a statement in such a matter-of-fact tone, yet the words struck home. This was not, after all, the world he knew. He was far from home in an ancient, haunted land, among killers. He wiped the sweat from his forehead, though they were in the relatively cool shadow of columns.

"What am I supposed to do when I get it?"

"I will tell you at that time."

"You don't have it with you?"

Said shook his head. "I do not carry such things about with me."

"How much is it worth?"

"The ruby in it is worth, I suppose, thirty or forty thousand pounds, about seventy thousand dollars As an antiquity, though, its value is many times greater."

Pete whistled. A thought occurred to him. "What good would it do somebody outside Egypt? I mean, they could never show it or resell it, because it's stolen property—stolen from the country, anyway."

Said smiled tolerantly. "You don't understand collectors. They will pay our price just to have the necklace. Also, in time, they can show the necklace and even resell it, saying that it was got out of Egypt before the law concerning antiquities was passed."

"You have a buyer?"

"Buyers," said Said. "There is some bidding going on right now in the United States. We will get a high price, never fear."

"What is your connection with Hastings and Hélène?"

"They are my employees."

This was a jolt. For some reason it had never occurred to Pete that the two Europeans were not the main figures in the plot. "I didn't know," said Pete.

"Why should you know?" Said was bland. "They are both discreet persons. We have been in business, off and on, for some years. Since 1940, as a matter of fact."

"During the war?"

"Business does not stop because people decide to kill one another on a large scale. If anything, business becomes even more interesting and profitable then."

Pete said nothing to that bit of wisdom. His whole original conception of this venture was obviously all wrong; he would have to begin again. "You live in Luxor?"

Said nodded. "I prefer it. I was born here, though I've traveled a good bit. Went to school in England, where I knew Hastings. First-rate athlete, by the way. Hard to believe now. I have since conducted a number of enterprises hereabouts, which have not all proved to be disappointing." He chuckled softly and with his sinewy brown hand caressed the carvings on the wall.

"When do I get the necklace?"

Said stared at him, or seemed to, his face made impassive by the dark glasses. "You are in a hurry?"

"A little bit. I want to get back to Cairo."

"To Hélène?"

"Yes, now you mention it." The lie came easily.

"I will give it to you tomorrow, perhaps later. There is no hurry at the moment."

"You mean you're sizing me up?"

"How well you put it! Yes, that is what I am doing."

"Afraid maybe I'll take off with it?"

"Not exactly." Said lit a Turkish cigarette, after offering one to Pete, who refused it. Delicate blue smoke curled upward between them for a brief moment. Said exhaled comfortably. "Put it this way: You might possibly want to get out of Egypt with our necklace, then again you might not. I have no way of knowing. I am hardly a psychologist. My one fault is that I am by nature trusting and I am often tricked." He removed a fleck of tobacco from his lower lip. Pete did not even pretend to be taken in by the other's pose of innocence.

"I am known to be an easy mark among the natives here," continued Said, obviously enjoying the image of himself as a

trusting fool. "But I do my best to get by, to defend my interests. That is why I am, as you call it, sizing you up. You see,
there is no reason why you shouldn't attempt to steal the
necklace. In your place, *I* would be tempted. But, knowing
certain things, I would also be cautious."

Now it was coming. "What things?"

"First, that the police are with us. It would not do to appeal
to them for protection."

"Protection? From what?"

"From me, Mr. Wells—assuming you try to double-cross
me."

"I'd hardly try that," said Pete, a little guiltily, for, against
his will, in the last few minutes he had considered the possibility of getting off with the treasure, selling it for himself,
for Anna. They could settle down on the proceeds. But it
had only been a sudden fantastic dream.

"I'm sure you wouldn't, because, I suspect, you're intelligent. I'm not trying to flatter you, but I can see why
Hélène sent you to me. You are quick. I like that. Even so, I
will tell you why you won't attempt to cut in on us for more
than the share of the proceeds we will give you."

This was good to hear, thought Pete, wondering if it was
true, if Said was serious. "You mean I'll get something on
top of what I'm getting now?"

"When the sale is completed, yes. But I was explaining to
you the reasons why I feel you will be too clever to try to
outwit us. In Egypt we have the police, as I have said, and
that is very important. Outside of Egypt we are connected
with an organization that I have no intention of discussing

with you. Only bear in mind that no matter where you are in the world, we have agents, and should you try anything unpleasant, you will be killed."

"I get you," said Pete, conscious of the sweat trickling down his side under the thin sport shirt he was wearing. He had a clearer idea of Said now. The tie-up was unexpected but logical. Said was obviously a member of an international crime syndicate, or connected with one for business reasons. He was almost certain, too, that the Egyptian was in the dope business and that smuggling antiquities was only a side line with him.

"I'm glad you do, Peter, if I may call you by your first name."

"Call me Pete." For some reason he wanted to keep the name Peter for Anna alone.

"Pete it is, then." Said smiled kindly. "I think we begin to understand each other."

"How far am I to go with the necklace?"

"To Europe, I think. That's all I can tell you for the moment. When the details have been worked out, Hélène will tell you. We will have no idea until we have accepted an offer, and that will take several days, at least. Meanwhile, you can enjoy yourself in Cairo."

"With a hundred thousand dollars' worth of jewelry on me? Not on your life."

Said laughed. "You won't be suspected."

"I already am." And Pete told him about his meetings with Mohammed Ali.

Said frowned. "It is not too bad, of course. The Inspector

is an old friend of ours. I think it unlikely he will try to take the necklace away from you. Be on your guard, though. Keep it with you all the time, or if you hide it, hide it well."

Then Pete asked about the one aspect of the plot that still mystified him.

"What's the point of roping me into this? Why can't you take the necklace yourself down to Cairo and get it out of Egypt? If you've taken care of the police, who are you worried about?"

The Egyptian's face set suddenly, involuntarily, but then, in a flash, it was relaxed again as he said, "It is our way. We need a courier, someone who can take care of himself. As for danger—well, there is plenty of it, and that's why we hired you. I can't tell you any more." And that was the end of that.

Said moved slowly now through the columns, Pete at his side. "The necklace has had an interesting history," said the Egyptian as they came out into the sun again and stood before an enormous obelisk, guarded by a small granite sphinx. "The Queen's original tomb was robbed over two thousand years ago; she was moved then to another tomb, already occupied. What jewelry was left her was inside the sarcophagus, on her body, the mummy. When the tomb was discovered, the necklace was stolen. It came into my hands quite a few years ago and I have kept it much too long."

"Too long?"

Said nodded gravely. "There is a curse on it, you see. The man who stole it from the tomb died horribly, burned alive in his bed. The next owner sold it to me after his wife and two children were killed in an automobile accident. He sold it to me for almost nothing, less than the value of the ruby, just to be rid of it. Poor fellow, he killed himself a month later." They were now walking down a long avenue lined with carved effigies of kings and gods. The sun was like a weight on Pete's head.

"But nothing's happened to you, has it?"

Said shook his head. "No, not yet. But I am superstitious, I fear, like all the rest. From the time we are children they tell us about the curse on the tombs. All of us who live here grow up knowing that evil befalls those who antagonize the old gods. It is in our bones. Lately I have been involved in some delicate affairs. I need luck. So it seemed as good a time as any to sell the necklace. I contacted Hastings and Hélène, who handle the Cairo end of our affairs, and told them to make arrangements to get the thing out of Egypt and into the hands of our American customer. You are the result."

"Is that O.K. by you?"

Said paused in the shadow of a statue of a fat, half-naked king. "Yes, I think it's O.K. by me," he said slowly. "I believe we can trust you, not because you are honest—there is never any way of telling, no matter what people claim—but because you're intelligent, and want to live."

"You make it sound real nice," said Pete, grinning.

"We'll get along," said Said. "But here's my car. Perhaps you'd like to honor my house with a visit?"

Pete said that he would. They got into the prewar Rolls Royce parked at the end of the avenue of statuary. The native chauffeur started the car and drove west.

Said's house was a long, white, rather unattractive building in the best Hollywood-Spanish style. It was set back in the desert, among date palms and tropical trees and flowers.

"I have an oasis to myself," said the Egyptian as they got out of the car and went into the house. The interior was more unusual. It was crammed full with expensive antique furniture, English and French, as well as many Egyptian pieces.

Said ushered him into a cool dim room that opened onto a terrace beyond, where, surrounded by palms, a fountain flowed into a large pond, the center of the oasis.

Pete sat down in a big chair overlooking the gardens. "Man, I'm glad to be out of that sun."

"Gin and tonic?" Pete said that that would suit him fine and Said clapped his hands. A houseboy appeared instantly and took the order. Said sat down opposite Pete. "It is peaceful here," he said pleasantly. "A little too peaceful for most people's taste, but I like it. And now that we have such good air service, it is possible to be in Rome or Paris in a few hours, which makes it less like being buried alive." While he talked, Pete looked about the room. He was particularly interested in the silver-framed photographs decorating many of the tables. There was one of the King and several of women in evening clothes, very elegant-looking, but the photograph that interested him most was the one nearest his chair: a tall man wearing a uniform with a girl on his arm. From where Pete sat their faces were indistinct; but the swastika on the man's coat sleeve was unmistakable.

Said, seeing he had noticed the picture, said, a little too

quickly, "Tactless, I suppose, but then the Nazis *were* all over Egypt a few years ago and many of us did do business with them. After all, to an Egyptian there is little difference between an English and a German soldier. Both are foreign. One conquered us and the other tried to. But it's certainly unfashionable now to say such things."

"Who are they?"

"The man was called Erich Raedermann. He was the chief Nazi in Cairo during the war. The girl is Hélène."

Pete looked at the photograph closely, curious to see what Hélène's dead lover was like. He seemed quite handsome, and she looked radiant and young. "He was shot, wasn't he?"

"In her arms. But you know the story."

"Yes, I've heard it." Their drinks were brought them.

Said apologized for drinking. "The Prophet will forgive me, I'm sure," he said, flashing the gold tooth. "My work is a great strain."

"I'm sure it is," said Pete, wondering what his work really was. He had a good idea, but it was only a guess; it was also none of his business. He asked how far it was to Aswân, and when Said wanted to know why he was interested in that dreary place, Pete told him a little about Anna.

Said was interested. "You know this girl?" he asked.

"I met her yesterday."

"She seems to have made a great impression on you."

"She is a remarkable girl."

"Quite pretty, too." Said smiled tolerantly. Then, for the first time, he removed his dark glasses, and Pete saw why he had worn them. One eye was a brilliant blue, startling for one so dark; the other eye was white, filmed with cataracts, and blind. Said rubbed his eyelids thoughtfully. He was completely unselfconscious. "I was under the impression that you were interested in Hélène."

"I suppose that's what she would say." Pete was a little irritated that she had discussed him, even with Said. It was, after all, a private matter, or should have been. But then Pete remembered that he had mentioned to him that the reason he wanted to get back to Cairo soon was to see her. "She's a little too high-powered for me."

"High-powered—what a good phrase! I see what you mean, but she is attractive, extremely so."

"So I thought," said Pete, taking a long swallow of the gin and tonic. "But I couldn't make much time with her."

"She's a difficult woman to know," said his host. "You will find that out for yourself, I suspect. But tell me about the German girl."

"I don't think there's much to tell. At least, *I* don't know much about her. She's a pretty exciting number, I'll say that." Purposely, advised by instinct, Pete sounded casual, spoke of her as just an ordinary good-looking girl who had come his way.

"I suspect you of being a Don Juan," said Said pleasantly.

"I take what I can get," said Pete, almost truthfully.

"It may be that I can keep you amused in Luxor, while the German girl is upriver. I have a fairly large selection of girls in Luxor. We are more simple about these things in Egypt than the Europeans and Americans are. Of course, the women who belong to families are taboo, but there are many others who are on their own and anxious to please. If you like, we might have a little party tomorrow evening."

Pete ducked that one vaguely. Ordinarily he would have jumped at the opportunity, but knowing Anna had somehow altered, for the time being at least, his usual desires. He wanted only her.

"Should you change your mind—" But he was not allowed to finish. A houseboy entered and whispered something in Said's ear. The Egyptian nodded curtly; the boy disappeared. "We have a visitor," he said. "Your friend Mohammed Ali."

Pete was startled. "What do you think he wants?"

"I should say, in general, he wants money. What he wants in particular *this* time, I don't know."

They both rose as the Inspector entered. Said, beaming warmly, greeted the policeman, "What a happy surprise this is! We see too little of you here at the oasis."

"Government duties, Said Pasha," said the Inspector, glancing at Pete without any sign of recognition.

"I believe you know Mr. Wells, Inspector." Pete shook hands; then all three sat down, the Inspector between Said and Pete.

Mohammed Ali accepted tea. After wiping his face with a large red handkerchief, he said, "I had forgotten, Pasha, how cool your house is."

"Through no fault of mine, Inspector," said their host silkily. "You are always an honored guest here."

"Kind, too kind," murmured the policeman, looking at Pete. "Tell me, Mr. Wells, did you finally locate Fräulein Mueller?"

"Locate her?" Pete stared at him innocently.

"Yes, I believe the manager told you she had gone to Aswân. He seemed to think you were planning to follow her."

"The manager jumps to conclusions," said Pete shortly.

"You would have enjoyed Aswân, Mr. Wells. Hot, of course, hotter than Luxor even, but an interesting place. It's the old Egypt."

"I'm seeing enough sights right now," said Pete.

"But not sights that include Fräulein Mueller."

Before Pete could answer, Said interrupted: "What is the political news, Inspector? I haven't been to Cairo in some weeks and the news travels slowly."

"Everything is quiet," said the Inspector, shifting his gaze from Peter to his host. "The usual talk of rebellions, nothing more."

"The King?"

"Enjoys good health."

"I am happy to hear that, very happy," said Said, bowing his head reverently.

"We protect his safety with our lives," said Mohammed Ali, glancing at Pete, who did not get the significance of this remark, if any was intended.

"Is there anything I can do for you, Inspector?" asked Said. "Your word is my command."

"Nothing, Pasha," said the policeman with a smile. "I was driving this way and I thought it would be good to see my old friend. I had no idea I should see the young American, too. A double pleasure."

Pete unconsciously doubled his fists in his lap. He disliked this man; they were enemies, though precisely why he could not tell. It was enough that the policeman had tried to come between him and Anna. He wondered how much the Inspector knew about last night, about where Anna had gone that morning. He made up his mind to find out as soon as possible.

They talked for a few minutes about the state of affairs in Egypt. Then Mohammed Ali rose and offered to take Pete back to Luxor. "It is nearly time for lunch at the hotel."

Pete glanced quickly at Said, who nodded imperceptibly. "Sure, thanks for the ride."

Said escorted them to the door. "A great honor, Inspector," he said, bowing. "I am happy to have met you, too, Mr. Wells. I hope we'll meet again."

The ride back to town was not cheerful. Mohammed Ali drove and Pete sat beside him. It was not until they were almost at the hotel that he asked, "Where is she?"

"Do you mean Fräulein Mueller?"

"That's exactly who I mean. Why'd she go to Aswân?"

"I should've thought she'd've told you, Mr. Wells—last night."

"What do you mean?"

Mohammed Ali smiled maliciously. "Haven't you noticed that all the rooms of our hotel have balconies? That it's possible to go from balcony to balcony by simply stepping from one to the next? They are less than a meter apart."

Pete flushed. "You were on her balcony?"

"For a little while. My room is nearby."

"And you watched us?"

"Heard is the better word, since the room was dark."

"You know what I'd like to do to you?"

"Something rash, I fear," said the policeman. "In this country, though, I, the police, do the doing—if that is good English."

"Maybe you have a surprise coming," said Pete, controlling his anger carefully. He would have plenty of time later on to take care of him. Meanwhile he must find Anna.

"I hope there will be *many* happy surprises," said the policeman, and he put his hand gently on Pete's knee.

"You're so right," said Pete, lifting the hand off his leg. For a single moment there was a trial of strength. Both men strained mightily. Pete won and the hand was removed.

Mohammed Ali was quite pale and sweat beaded his forehead. "You are strong," he said. "I like that."

"Where is she?"

"How should I know? I presume she is in Aswān."

"Why are you interested in her?"

"For reasons that don't concern you, Mr. Wells. If they did…well, I hope they will not. But here's the hotel." He parked the car in the driveway and together they went into the lobby.

Osman was waiting for Pete beside the desk. He flashed his usual canine grin and said, "Here is the package, Sir Wells," and he handed Pete a small but heavy cardboard box. "We go to see sights maybe tomorrow," and in a rustle of robes he was gone. Peter pocketed the box quickly, aware of Mohammed Ali's interested gaze. He asked the manager if there had been any word from Anna.

"No, sir, nothing. I am sure she'll be back soon, though.

She took only a small handbag with her; her clothes are still in her room." He chattered on but Pete turned away, suddenly worried, afraid.

Mohammed Ali walked with him to the dining room. "I must leave you here," he said pleasantly. "Perhaps we can have dinner together tonight. Unless, of course, you decide to go to Aswân."

But Pete had no intention of going there. He spent the afternoon telephoning the hotels of Aswân, with no success. No one named Anna Mueller was registered at any of them. There was a chance she had gone to stay with friends, if she had gone at all. The fact that the Inspector had seemed anxious for him to leave Luxor made him suspect she was somewhere else…perhaps in the hands of the police.

The box Osman had given him contained a small German revolver and several ammunition clips. Just owning this compact weapon made him more cheerful. He decided that if he had not heard from Anna in twenty-four hours he would begin his own investigation, and Mohammed Ali would find it thorough, he thought, his lips setting in a hard line.

He had dinner that night alone. The policeman was nowhere in sight.

Dinner over, Pete lit a cigarette and strolled out of the hotel. The night was magnificent. The sky was black as ink and the stars were bright and clear. An enormous moon shone, white and full. A warm breeze stirred the palm trees. Pete wanted Anna then, more than he had ever wanted anything in his life.

Lonely, worried, he crossed the street and stood looking

down at the Nile, which shone dull silver in the moonlight.
From far away he could hear laughter in the town, the noise
of traffic in the narrow streets.

"The good night, Sir Wells," said a voice behind him.

He turned quickly and saw Osman standing behind him.
He resembled a jackal, thought Pete suddenly, not liking the
way the other's eyes shone in the moonlight. "What are you
doing here?" he asked.

"I am come to talk with Sir Wells."

"About what?"

"The pale lady he likes," said Osman, smiling.

"You mean Anna Mueller."

"Her name, yes."

"What about her?"

"I know where to find her if Sir Wells looks for her."

"Where the hell is she, then?"

"In the tombs," said Osman.

Pete grew cold. "She's dead?"

"No, not dead. Across the river, there." And he waved a
long hand toward the low white hills webbed with shadow.

"How do you know she's there?"

"Because I heard her tell manager of hotel she goes across
the river for a few days, to the Libyan Inn. Small place up
near the tombs."

Pete grabbed the old man suddenly by the gown and drew
him close to him, so close he could smell Osman's world odor.
"You lying to me?" he said, his voice low but harsh.

"No, Sir Wells," said the old man. "She goes there." He
looked into Pete's eyes fearlessly.

Pete let him go, a little ashamed of himself. "Why didn't you tell me this sooner?"

"Because you first must see Said Pasha. Tonight I speak not, because Mohammed Ali is with you. When I hear manager say the pale lady goes to Aswân, I know they tell lies."

"Is there a telephone over there?"

"No, Sir Wells. It is small place. Few of the Europeans go there."

"How do we get across the river?"

"Now? So late in the night?"

"Yes, now. Right now." The moon might not be wasted yet.

Osman shrugged. "It is possible we can rent small boat to take us across, Sir Wells. But it is late."

"Come on."

Reluctantly Osman led him down the cliff to the water's edge. It was a difficult scramble because there were no steps at this point, only a stony slope covered with sun-withered brush. At the bottom of the cliff they stood among the jagged rocks that edged the shrunken river.

Osman looked about him carefully, like an animal trying to catch a scent. In the silence, Pete was aware of life all about them.

A few yards away a group of naked men bathed in the river, silently, hardly rippling the water, the moon glinting on their dark bodies like light on metal. Here and there along the riverbank small yellow fires gleamed, and about them figures sat, eating and murmuring together in the breathy Arab dialect.

"We must find honest one," said Osman finally, moving

southward, threading his way between the rocks, Pete close behind.

"Honest what?"

"Boatman. Many are thieves, and at night is danger." As they walked Pete saw many small boats moored to the rocks.

The first boatman Osman found proved unsatisfactory: a powerful, bearded man who sat alone by a tiny fire, his boat close by. After sharp words, they moved on. The second boatman, a young boy, proved more satisfactory and he was hired for the equivalent of two dollars.

The boat was an old dinghy, its bottom much tarred. Even so, a few minutes after they pushed off water began to seep in through cracks at their feet. The boy paid no attention. He rowed intensely, quietly, the only sound that of his breathing.

"Not much of a boat," said Pete in a low voice.

"It will get us there," said Osman, sitting back in the stern.

Pete let his hand trail in the water. It was warm, warmer than he had suspected. He watched the lights of Luxor recede as they approached the western shore, a much darker shore, he noticed, with fewer lights.

"How far is it from the shore to the inn?" he asked.

"Almost five kilometers."

"That's quite a ways. Is there any kind of carriage on the other side?"

"Not now. We walk," said Osman cheerfully.

The boat landed on the western bank just as the water had begun to get seriously deep in the bottom. Pete hopped ashore, followed more sedately by the dragoman.

There followed, then, a quarrel between Osman and the

boy. The burden of it, Pete discovered, had to do with the boy's waiting for them on that side of the river.

"He is superstitious," said Osman contemptuously, "afraid of evil spirits. I tell him he must wait."

"Not for me. I'll spend the night at the inn."

"But for me," said Osman. "I wish to go back this night to Luxor."

Pete solved the problem like Solomon; he tore a piaster note in half and gave it to the boy. "Tell him you'll give him the other half when he takes you back."

This delighted Osman; the boy complained loudly, finally bursting into tears and tearing his hair in the best Arab tradition, but they were firm and left him sitting on the bank.

"He will wait," said Osman confidently, as they walked up the embankment to the road.

The road was a winding one, very dusty and rutted from cartwheels. It wound in and out among groves of olive trees. The land on this side of the river was rolling, not flat like the eastern side. They walked a long time without speaking. Occasionally a muffled figure would pass them on the road, silent, swift-moving, and involuntarily Pete's hand would go to the revolver in his pocket. Osman noticed this.

"Very wise, Sir Wells. Many thieves on these roads at night. They kill so easy." And he chuckled, an unpleasant sound.

Pete felt better when they had left the tree-lined section of the road and moved up into the hills, into an open stretch of land where the road was straight. No ambush on this road, he thought, looking to left and right at the farmhouses

across the dry stubbled fields crisscrossed with narrow ditches
containing stagnant river water.

They did not pause until they reached the end of this
straight road, when, huge in the night, two enormous statues
loomed, the largest Pete had ever seen, one on each side of
the road. It was an uncanny sight, in the silver glare.

"What the hell are those things?" he asked, standing at
the base of one of the statues. Both were alike: a seated man
wearing the royal headdress of ancient Egypt.

"The Colossi, Sir Wells," said Osman, assuming his professional guide's voice. "Among the wonders of the world,
builded by the great king Amenhotep to his glory."

So clear was the light that Pete could even make out the
face of the dead king, a heavy face with a curiously gentle
smile that made him uneasy, as though the smile were
meant for him: a warning.

"Let's get going," he said, lowering his voice for no reason
as they walked between the statues toward the low hills bor-
dering sharp cliffs.

Half a mile beyond the statues they came to a village of
mud huts, forty or fifty shacks placed haphazardly on the top
of one of the hills. Even before they actually saw the village,
they could smell it: wood smoke, urine, goats—the usual
odors of an Arab community.

Osman was nervous, Peter could see, and he wondered
why. It was understandable on the road, unprotected, at the
mercy of hidden thieves, but here in civilization, relatively
speaking, they were safe.

"Please to be quiet," whispered Osman, leading the way

through the huts, keeping away from the central ones, which circled a fire at which many of the native men were gathered, though the night was warm. There was no sign of electricity anywhere. The lighted hovels contained only flickering candles or weak lanterns.

They moved unnoticed through the outskirts of the village.

But then, almost free of the last irregular row of huts, Pete stepped on a soft dark shape that, by its hair-raising yowl, turned out to be a child asleep in the street.

There was wild confusion. The child ran screaming toward the center of the village. Women, unveiled for the night, appeared in doorways. Men came rushing toward them, their robes billowing behind them, firebrands in their hands.

"Quick!" Osman pulled Pete after him. They leaped off the hill's summit and into a shallow ravine. Breathless, a little stunned by the impact, Pete limped after Osman, who was heading up the ravine, just as the light of torches fell across them from above and a high shouting began as the excited Arabs sighted strangers.

Pete followed Osman, thankful for the moonlight, stumbling over boulders as they made their way among a maze of ravines cut out of the limestone hill. In a few minutes they were out of range of the villagers, though they could still hear the shouting as the men searched the ravine they had just left.

Finally, at the mouth of what looked like a cave, Osman stopped, breathing heavily. "We...safe," he gasped. "No follow...here." They sat for some minutes on the dusty stone, resting.

Pete looked up at the huge black sky, speckled with brilliant stars. He had the sensation of lying at the bottom of a trench, of a grave, even; for in this place there was almost no vegetation, only porous white limestone, pale as bones in the moonlight.

Finally, when he could breathe easily, Pete asked, "Where are we?"

"Among the tombs," said the old man.

Pete looked about him. Farther down the ravine in which they sat, he could see two more oblong openings, like the one immediately behind them. "Those?" he asked, pointing to one of the caves.

Osman nodded. "Not the kings, though. Rich men, nobles are buried here. Long ages ago the tombs are sealed, but Europeans come and open them and steal the treasures." There was an unexpected note of bitterness in the old man's voice.

"Where are the kings?"

"In a valley to the west of here. We see it in daytime perhaps."

"Why did they chase us?"

Osman shrugged. "It is night. They are afraid. They hate strangers, and white men, and bad spirits."

"They thought we were ghosts?"

"Who knows? The torches they carried are supposed to keep them from harm at the hands of the dead."

"The dead," repeated Peter thoughtfully.

"Now we must go on to the inn. It is longer journey now."

Osman got to his feet slowly. Pete did the same. He was surprised to find that he was cold, though he had been running and the night was warm, like a dark soft blanket all about them.

Osman led him through a labyrinth of similar ravines. Several acres, perhaps more, of limestone had been worn away by some forgotten flood, leaving behind a series of confusing trenches, a dozen feet deep, containing the tombs of the old Egyptians.

It was a strange sensation, like walking in a roofless corridor, for the steep bare slopes were like walls, and the world above, except for the black sky, was no longer visible. There was no sound but the heavy echo of their footsteps and the distant yapping of wild dogs.

Eternity passed and still there was no end to it. Pete kept his eye on the North Star and discovered soon enough that Osman was off course. They were heading southwest instead of northeast

He stopped; the old man turned around. "Sir Wells is tired?" He spoke in his ordinary voice and the sound of it was as loud as a shot.

"Shut up," whispered Pete furiously.

"There is no danger now," said the other, lowering his voice.

"We're going in the wrong direction. We're going south."

Osman nodded, undisturbed. "It is so. We must go backward to go forward in the tombs."

"Then why don't we climb out of here and get back on the road? There *is* a road, isn't there?"

"Of course, Sir Wells, but we are miles away from it now. We are above the Libyan Inn. We move south toward it. We are safest in the tombs, because no Egyptians will come here at night, fearing them," and he gestured with one long hand at the dark entrance nearest them, a narrow doorway in the rock perhaps five feet tall.

"Why aren't *you* afraid?" asked Pete, and he lit a cigarette, soothed suddenly by the taste of American tobacco.

"I am educated man," said Osman stiffly. "I do not fear such things. Besides," he added, holding up a small pendant that he wore about his neck inside his robe, "I wear this. Annubis, god of the dead, protects me." His wide, long-toothed smile gleamed in the pale light as Pete perfunctorily examined the tiny figure of the hawk-headed god.

"How much longer will it take?" he asked as they began their journey again, Osman leading the way nimbly over fallen rock. There was not room enough in most places for two men to walk abreast.

"An hour, Sir Wells, no more." He cocked his head skyward at the moon and said, "Soon she will be gone."

"The moon?"

"Yes. It will be difficult to travel then, in the dark. You have no light?"

"Only a cigarette lighter, which isn't much use," said Pete.

Osman stroked his chin thoughtfully. "Perhaps the dark is better. Stars give light." He paused. "What was that?" he whispered, fear in his voice.

Pete strained but could hear nothing. He was about to say something when the old man silenced him with a gesture.

"Quick!" he whispered. "In here." And he ducked into one of the caves. Pete followed him.

He was forced to crouch a little to get inside the door, but once inside he could stand erect with ease. He lifted one hand and touched the smooth stone overhead; the ceiling was only a few inches above his head.

He could hear Osman breathing hoarsely beside him in the blackness. He tried to say something but the old man snorted softly, warningly. They stood for several long minutes in the dark close chamber. Then Osman whispered, "Light."

Pete fumbled through his pockets until he found his cigarette lighter. He snapped it on. To his surprise the walls were brilliant with paintings, as bright and glowing as they had been three thousand years before. Every inch of wall was painted. At the end opposite the door by which they had entered was another, smaller opening.

Osman looked out into the ravine. Satisfied, he turned to Pete. "All is well," he said.

"What did you hear?"

"I thought I heard the men walking, but I was wrong." He grinned in the flaring light and pointed to the door at the back of the chamber. "It is there they place the mummy."

Pete shuddered. "Let's get the hell out of here." A warm blast of air snuffed out his lighter. He cursed sharply and lit it again, just as a tall figure stepped through the door of the burial room, the face shrouded in a robe.

Osman shrieked harshly like a frightened parrot. The lighter went out again. Pete made a dash for the door, striking his head in a sharp blow that made him reel. Clutching his fore-head, momentarily blinded, he staggered out into the ravine.

Then they were upon him.

At first he could not tell how many they were. He fought blindly, swinging wildly from left to right, striking hard flesh and bone with his fists while hands clutched at him, tried to throw him off balance.

His head cleared as he struggled. He was able to break clear for a moment, and in that moment he saw three men in Arab dress closing in on him.

In the moonlight the knife that one was carrying flashed against the black sky.

He ran. But it was no use. Rocks tripped him. He stumbled, fell, got to his feet; then they had him surrounded, were closing in on him.

He fought desperately but they were too heavy. They overpowered him with the weight of their bodies, heavy Arab bodies swathed in robes. He got only a blurred impression of the faces. All were strangers to him, dark, big-nosed men with black gleaming eyes.

Two of them held him on his back, their bodies like stones on his chest, holding him flat to the ground though he still twisted and fought, his arms pinioned at his sides. The third man stood over him for a moment, and then, with a hard hand, struck him across the face. His neck cracked. Stars swam in his head and for a moment he nearly lost consciousness; but then, with an effort, he brought his eyes into focus again. The slap had suddenly cleared his brain. He was no longer an unreasoning trapped animal. He stopped struggling.

"What do you want?" he asked, his own voice sounding far away in his ears.

The Arab who had hit him only grunted. He was going through his pants pockets.

"I haven't got much money," said Pete, "but…" As he talked to them, he found he could move his right hand. The Arab holding him on that side lay across his arm and shoulder, but his hand and wrist were left free. It was in the right-hand coat pocket of his jacket that he had put the pistol. Carefully, stealthily, he moved his hand toward the revolver, talking all the time, promising them money if they let him go.

The Arab who had been searching him muttered something to the others. For a second he was afraid they would search his jacket before he could get his hand to the gun, but they were no longer interested in robbing him. The two men holding him threw their weight even more heavily on his chest and belly, holding his arms tight under them. This shift in position brought Pete's hand closer to the revolver. With a sudden move, he could get to it and fire. With the tips of his fingers he felt the hard metal. His hand was already in the pocket.

When he saw what the Arab was doing, though, he froze in terror, the revolver forgotten.

The man had taken out his long knife and, with a professional twist, cut Pete's belt in two. The other two got a scissors grip on his legs as his trousers were opened. Then the man raised his knife hand and in a flash of light brought it down.

The rest was confusion. Pete gave a blood-curdling yell and with all his strength grabbed the pistol, firing it without aiming. The shot was like thunder echoing in the stone ravine.

The Arab with the knife stepped back, startled. One man shrieked and the other leaped to his feet. Pete fired again, under cover of the wounded Arab. The one with the knife grasped his belly with both hands; the third scrambled up the side of the ravine and was gone.

Pete shoved clear of the dead man who lay across him. In the moonlight, blood flowed black upon the stone. He got to his feet quickly and, taking careful aim, fired two more shots into the crouched figure of the Arab opposite him. The man rocked back and forth gently and then, with a sound of retching, fell face downward on the ground.

For a long moment Pete stood dazed between the two dead men, his breath coming in great gasps and his head swimming. He was afraid he might be sick, but the nausea passed.

He sat down shakily on a boulder and examined the inside of his thigh where the Arab's knife had cut him. The blood was flowing fast but the cut, he saw, was not deep, only a scratch. He wadded his handkerchief over the wound and tied it fast with the remains of his belt.

Then, just as he was about to search the dead Arabs, the moon set and the darkness suddenly closed in about him, warm and protecting. By starlight, the white stone glowed dully, and all objects were indistinct and vague against it.

When the bleeding had stopped a little, he got to his feet and climbed, very carefully, the wall of the gully.

He found himself in unfamiliar country. The mountains

were close by; the river was at least a dozen miles away. Luxor was a blur of light in the distance, north of where he stood.

Finally he made out, some miles to the south, a cluster of darkened buildings circling a larger one with lighted windows. The light shone steadily: electric light. Since this was the only sign of civilization on his side of the river, he headed toward it, walking slowly over fields of stubble, across shallow irrigation trenches filled with stinking mud and water.

Occasionally he would see figures moving, but when he called out to them to ask his way, they fled without answer into the shadows.

The sky was gray with morning when he reached the Libyan Inn.

Chapter Five

Pete collapsed onto the bed, hardly aware of what was happening. From far away he could hear Anna moving about the room, but even the sting of iodine on his leg did not arouse him. Without a word, he fell asleep. He did not open his eyes again until late afternoon. She was standing beside the bed with a tray of food. She smiled. "You haven't moved for hours," she said, putting the tray down beside the bed.

"Hours?" he repeated stupidly, his mind still fogged with sleep. He was conscious that the room was hot, that he was sweating uncomfortably. He sat up and she placed a pillow behind him. "What time is it?"

"Nearly four. Come, eat this. You must be weak. I think you lost a lot of blood."

He glanced at his thigh where the bandage covered the scratch. His trouser leg was stiff with dried blood. He moved his leg carefully, flexing the muscles. Everything worked properly, though there was a soreness about the wound.

Anna sat down on the edge of the bed while he ate. "You gave the inn a great surprise," she said. "They wanted to know if they should call the police."

"What did you say?"

"I said it was up to you."

"Do you think they did?"

"I think so. Does it matter?" She looked at him directly, her blue eyes serious.

He shook his head. "No, I guess not. I object to the attention but that can't be helped."

"What happened, Peter?"

He told her, as best he could. Already the wild chase in the tombs seemed like a nightmare only half remembered. She listened intently. When he had finished, unable to recall exactly how he'd got to the inn from the tombs, she asked the obvious question: Had it been planned?

"I don't know," he said wearily. "I haven't any idea. I don't think the trouble in the village was planned. I mean it was because I stepped on that kid that they started after us, thinking we were evil spirits."

"But I wonder, Peter, if it was necessary to go through the village at all."

He hadn't thought of this. "I'm not sure. I was pretty vague about the geography. I figured Osman knew where he was going."

"We'll look at a map later," said Anna. She was suddenly shrewd and capable. He had never thought of her like this, but then he remembered how she had been forced to live, by her wits. There was nothing weak or hesitant about her in a crisis.

"Good plan. We'll also have a better idea when we get back across the river and find out what happened to…that old devil."

"Why would they want to kill you?" asked Anna in a matter-of-fact voice, as though it were perfectly natural that there were people in the world who intended to kill him.

He chuckled nervously and handed the tray back to her. "You got me there," he said. "Later on, maybe, when I have something they want, but not now."

"Perhaps they don't want you to get the thing they want in the first place."

"Something in that." But he was already thinking back to the day before, to the manager at the Karnak Inn, to Mohammed Ali, to what each had said. "Tell me." he asked suddenly. "Why did you come over here?"

She looked away, pretended to arrange the dishes on the tray. "I had to," she said softly.

"You mean you were ordered to?"

"Yes…no. Oh, Peter, don't ask me about it yet. I can't tell you."

"Did you tell the manager at the inn that you had gone to Aswân?"

She shook her head. "I don't think I told him anything."

That cleared that up, at least, he thought grimly.

"You didn't want me to follow you?"

"No, Peter."

"You were afraid of me?"

"Not of you, my darling." She looked him full in the eyes. "I was afraid of falling in love. I was afraid of what might happen to you because of me."

"Like last night?"

"Perhaps like last night. I don't know about that."

"You think some of your Cairo friends might have got in my way?"

She looked away miserably. "I can't tell, but you shouldn't have come. I was only going to stay here a day or two, just long enough to think."

"To think?"

"About us, Peter. I wanted to be by myself, to make up my mind about so many things. I'm caught." She said this last abruptly, sharply, desperately. "I can't save myself or you or anything at all."

"We can get out of the country, Anna." He pulled her toward him and their lips met, his passionate and hers oddly passive, as though she had no strength left for loving. He was immediately conscious of this; he let go of her. "You don't care," he said.

She ran her hand gently over his face. "Care is not the word," she said softly. "But I do care, very much, too much for your sake. I don't want you killed."

"I don't think I will be," he said with more confidence than he felt. "Now will you tell me what you're mixed up in?"

"Soon," she said distractedly. "Very soon, I hope."

"Are *you* in any danger? I mean because of the mess you're in?"

She smiled. "What a funny word—mess. It means trouble, doesn't it? No, there is no real danger for me yet. But you must get dressed." She got to her feet. "The manager found a pair of trousers and a shirt that should fit you. You feel all right, don't you? Well enough to walk?"

He grinned. "I wouldn't be here now if I hadn't been up to a little walking last night." He swung his legs over the side of the bed. For a moment a dizzying green flood engulfed his eyes. He leaned forward, letting the blood rush to his head. When the room came into proper focus, he stood up. Except for a stiffness in his legs, he felt all right.

While he showered in the antique bathroom, he tried to think of ways for Anna and himself to leave Egypt, but each time a plan presented itself, lack of money made it impractical. He would have to find some way of getting hold of enough dollars to get them out before trouble really started, and serious trouble, he was sure, was about to begin for both of them. The business about the necklace was much too complicated to be successful. Too many people knew about it; too many people wanted it. He had become, almost without being aware of it, a target. A goddamned sitting duck, he muttered to himself as he turned off the water and stepped onto the tile floor of the dusty bathroom.

"What did you say?" Anna appeared in the doorway carrying the shirt and trousers.

"I was talking to myself. I was telling myself that if we didn't get out of here soon there was a good chance we'd stay here forever. Jackal bait, as they say."

Anna smiled. "We have time," she said, and she handed him a towel. While he dried himself and shaved with an old-fashioned razor she had found for him, they talked of the future, of what America was like. "In fact, I might even settle down and go to work," he said, putting on the clothes. They nearly fitted.

"Wild-dogging?"

He laughed. "Maybe that, too. Wildcatting is the word. But I don't want to. That's a single man's game, something for the adventure-loving boy."

"And you're not that sort of boy now?"

He pulled her toward him. "Just loving now," he said, and this time she returned his embrace, her hands caressing his back.

"Good evening," said Mohammed Ali. They turned quickly and saw the Inspector, standing in the doorway. "I couldn't be more disturbed over your accident."

Pete grunted as they moved, all three, into the bedroom and sat down. Anna was pale and distracted, twisting a handkerchief in her hands, the knuckles white with strain. Pete was more relaxed, or at least managed to appear to be. "How come you're here, Inspector?"

"I am the police," said Mohammed Ali simply. "Whenever a crime has been committed, we go. It is our duty."

"And maybe, when there's no crime, you commit it yourself?"

"Ah, Mr. Wells, you are so ungenerous!" He lit a cigarette with a flourish. Then: "I was notified a few hours ago that an American had been attacked last night in the tombs. I knew immediately who it was and so I came as quickly as possible. We wouldn't like anything to happen to you, Mr. Wells."

"I'm sure of that," said Pete.

"Now, to be businesslike for a moment." The Inspector pulled a small loose-leaf notebook from his tunic pocket.

With a pencil stub he made some marks in it. Then, in a precise neutral voice, he asked for details.

Pete gave them to him, amused by this official display. He did not exactly suspect Mohammed Ali of having made a trap for him the night before, but he was fairly confident that a man with so much information, so many irons in the fire, would probably know all he needed to know about events that interested him, and the movements of Pete Wells these days were obviously of a good deal of interest to the Inspector.

When the interrogation was finished, Pete asked about Osman.

The Inspector looked blank for a moment.

"The dragoman. He was the one who took me here, across the Nile. The old man I've just been telling you about."

The Inspector made another mark in his book. "You didn't tell me it was Osman," he said. "I know him. A fine old chap."

"Well, just tell me what happened to that fine old chap. The last I saw of him, he was streaking down a ravine headed for the river."

"I will find out for you."

"You mean you haven't seen him? He hasn't got in touch with you about last night?"

Mohammed Ali shook his head. "No, I learned about the accident from the hotel people here. They telephoned police headquarters in Luxor. By chance I was in the building when the call came through."

"And here you are."

"And here I am, in the room of the lovely Fräulein Mueller," and he nodded cordially in the direction of Anna, making the ghost of a salaam with his right hand. She looked away quickly.

"She was good enough to put me up this morning," said Pete coolly, "when I came here, bleeding like a stuck pig—"

"You look well now."

"Thank you. I don't feel it."

"I can understand," said the Inspector amiably, "You were in a bad situation. As far as I know, you are the first man in a long time to escape."

"To escape what?"

"The local people when they perform their…specialty. They work quickly. They take a knife, and then slash, it is done."

"Stop it," said Anna, suddenly white.

"The lips are then sewn shut," said Mohammed Ali, ignoring her, "and the man is left to die."

Pete felt sick to his stomach. "The point, though—what's the point to it?"

"Just a custom. Robbery is the motive, of course. It always is among the poor. The rest is an added refinement that goes back to the beginning of our culture."

Pete muttered an opinion of that culture, which the Inspector chose not to hear.

Mohammed Ali rose to go. "Said will be pleased to hear that you are safe," he said, politely.

"Did you find the bodies, by the way? Two were killed, I think, and the third got away."

"There are no bodies in Egypt," said the Inspector, smiling, "except the mummies in the tombs. I suggest you both return tomorrow to Luxor, where you will be better protected." He paused as though about to say something more, then, deciding not to, he bowed and left them alone.

"That devil!" said Anna, her voice sharp with strain.

The Libyan Inn was a cube of adobe surrounded by palm trees. It was nearly empty and they had the gloomy bare dining room to themselves. The manager, a fat, silent man with blue jowls, said, "Good evening," and nothing more, no comment about the attack or about the visit of Mohammed Ali.

They drank great quantities of a sweet Italian wine, and after a while, despite the stickiness of the wine, they grew more cheerful, less aware of their isolation in this remote and hostile country.

They talked of one another. She told him about her life before the war, about her family. "I was ashamed," she said thoughtfully. "Ashamed of my father even then, before I knew better, before Germany was defeated. He was good to me, in his way, and I adored him for a long time, until the last of the war. You see, they gave him a post at Dachau and he took it and was very successful there. The day Hitler killed himself, Father received a promotion in the S.S." She laughed bitterly. "I remember, though, wondering what it was that Father did. I knew that the camp was full of bad people, enemies of our country. We were very patriotic in those days. But I had no idea how the people in the camp were treated. Father told us very little about it. We lived in the town and seldom did we ever go to see him at work. I only remember going there once before the end and I thought it nice, very clean and neat, and the prisoners I saw, though terribly thin, looked like almost anyone else. It was that—the looking like everyone else—that first made me wonder."

"Wonder?"

"That something was wrong when so many ordinary people were locked up like that. I asked my father only once about it, and he was furious and struck me, very hard." She touched her face lightly, as though the pain lingered. "Then, when it was all over, the whole crazy dream, we were taken, all the people, children too, who lived in the town on a tour through the camp, and my God, what it was like!" She bit her lip suddenly at the memory.

"And your father?"

"He was hanged, after a trial."

"Were you sorry?"

"Only for my mother. She wept as though he had been good."

"Perhaps he had been, to her."

Anna shrugged. "Perhaps. I'm not sure. I forgot everything after that day when I walked through the camp and saw what my father had done."

"He might've been only a soldier, doing what he was told to do."

Anna was grim. "They all said that, but there were many

other kinds of duty for a soldier. You see, he asked for this place; he wanted to be like a little king. It all came out at the trial—the letters he wrote begging for the appointment, the letters afterward about what he was doing. Oh, it was disgusting!"

"But it's over now."

"Over?" He couldn't tell by her voice what she meant. He asked her about her mother. "She died a year after the execution. There was no point in her living in a world without Nazis."

"Did you hate her so?"

Anna shook her head. "No, I hated no one. Only the world that made my father into an animal, a killer." She paused; then she smiled. "I didn't want to talk about all that with you, ever. I promised myself I'd never tell you, and now look! How bored you must be!"

Pete shook his head. "I don't know how you lived through it. Afterward, I mean, when the crack-up came."

"I think it was easier, though," she said thoughtfully. "At least there was a kind of freedom. And I was lucky…to look nice, that is." The simple way she said this was like a cold knife in his chest. He changed the subject, not wanting to know more.

"I guess I had as different a time as it's possible to have," said Pete, and he told her what it was like living in Oregon in the thirties. Even the depression seemed like fun compared to her childhood.

"I had a good time. Maybe that was the trouble—too good a time. I didn't want to settle down, go to mining school like my brothers. I liked the idea of moving around, without any boss or place I had to be. So I started looking for oil. More a game, I guess, because even before the war it was no game for a guy without money, but I made a living, working every now and then for some big outfit. Then, once or twice, I got into some traffic—that's the word they used for smuggling. I was tied up with a gang in Juarez for a while. We'd smuggle damn near anything into the country from Mexico: gold, dope, wetbacks—that's the local word for Mexican laborers who get across the river into the States against the law, to work in Texas."

"Did you like that?" she asked. "Being a bandit?"

He grinned. "Well, it's a funny thing, but while I was doing it I never thought about it much one way or the other. I was having a good time and I was making money. It was like stealing home from third base in a baseball game. At the time it seemed like fun. The government had made a lot of border rules that seemed silly when you thought about them, and we had a chance to break the rules and make a little money as well as keep a lot of people happy. I know it was a dumb way to look at things, but at twenty-two you aren't apt to worry too much."

"They could have put you in jail, though."

"I expect they could, but before that happened I had figured out that it was all wrong the way I was living, so I went into partnership with a couple of other fellows and we even managed to make some money out of oil, which I spent. When it was gone I went into the Army. The war had started conveniently at that moment. I was in the Infantry for a long time, over four years, right until the end. I covered a lot of Europe on foot."

"You were brave?"

He chuckled. "As a matter of fact, I was. I was made a second lieutenant on the field, which was nearly as good as being shot by a firing squad, because second lieutenants got eaten up more than anybody else in that war. But I lived through it, getting medals for staying alive."

"I wish I had known you then."

He paused, suddenly serious. "It's just as good now, baby. We can start just as though nothing ever happened to either of us—as if I was always a real honest kid from Oregon and you…well, as though the roof hadn't fallen in on Germany."

Tears filmed her eyes. "But it did fall in, Peter." She bit her lip.

"Let's get out of here."

Together they went upstairs to her room. Since the manager had said nothing about arrangements for the night, Pete locked the door behind him and, in the bright moonlight, they lay together for a long time, not speaking, not thinking.

The next morning they were rowed back across the Nile. A tattered umbrella protected them from the huge fiery sun, which hung like an orange balloon in the pale sky. No clouds obscured it; there was no relief except the umbrella.

"I don't know how they stand it," said Pete, pointing to the boy who was rowing them, a tall youth with a dirty cloth cap on his head.

"It burns my eyes," she said, looking away.

"Are you getting tired of Egypt?" He smiled.

She laughed. "There are times when I long for a cold wet day with a gray sky and no sun at all."

"You'll like Oregon."

"Perhaps," she said, trailing her fingers in the warm water of the river.

They were greeted enthusiastically by the hotel manager, who crossed the lobby with hands outstretched, as though to embrace them both. "You are both safe! How worried we were when the Inspector told us what had happened! You were foolish, Mr. Wells, very foolish to go out alone like that, and near the tombs, where all the bandits are."

"I wasn't alone," said Pete, but the manager was busy relaying messages to Anna: There were two letters for her and she was to telephone Cairo that evening, someone of great importance had called and the manager's hands shook with excitement as he handed her the telephone message. Without looking at it she crumpled it into her pocket. Then she turned to Pete.

"I've got so many things to do, Peter," she said. "Shall we meet in the dining room tonight, at dinner?"

"Sure, if you want to." He tried to disguise his disappointment. For some reason he had thought they would be together all day, every day now. He had forgotten for a moment that they were, after all, separate, not tied to one another. "I hope you won't disappear again."

She smiled. "I'll warn you next time."

"I'll see you. Eight o'clock," he said, and she nodded; then she was gone.

Pete went to his own room. Everything was in order. He sat down on the edge of the bed and stripped his revolver, cleaned it, reloaded it. While he was doing this, the telephone rang.

"Mr. Wells?" asked a familiar voice. "This is Said."

"Oh. Hello there."

"I understand you had an adventure across the river night before last."

"That's one way of putting it. You nearly lost an errand boy."

Said chuckled. "They're not easily come by, either. Could you come to my house now?"

Pete said he would be there. After he hung up, he slid the revolver inside his belt on the left side, the butt at an angle where it could be easily reached. He had had little experience with small firearms. In the Army it had been an M-1 rifle all the time, but the principle was the same in any case: speed. Then he slipped on his gabardine jacket and went downstairs.

He looked about him as he left the hotel, half expecting to see Osman standing in his usual position beneath the acacia tree, but only a fat naked child sat there in the heat, listlessly playing in the sand.

A taxicab drove him at what seemed great speed across Luxor to the oasis of Said. His employer was waiting for him in the study overlooking the fountain. He was dressed, as before, in white. His dark glasses had been discarded and the one brilliant blue eye was turned always toward Pete, giving him suddenly the look of one of those figures in profile carved on the walls of the old temples.

"Too early in the day for a drink? Yes? No?" Pete ordered Scotch and it was brought by one of the silent white-clad boys who moved barefoot about the house. They sat then in silence, looking at one another while Pete drank, slowly, carefully, not because he wanted the whiskey but because he wanted to be doing something, to avoid the bright stare of that one blue eye.

At last Said spoke. "Why did you go across the river?"

"To see Anna Mueller."

"Didn't you realize how dangerous it was?"

"No, I'm afraid I didn't. Besides, I was with Osman. I figured he knew what to do if there was any trouble. He did, too. He ran like hell."

"Not fast enough," said the Egyptian.

"Why? Didn't he make it?"

"I think not. We have heard no word from him and that means just one thing."

"He was caught?"

"There is no other explanation." Said turned his good eye thoughtfully toward the garden. "He should have known better, I suppose. The error was his, not yours."

"I'm sorry," said Pete, wondering whether or not to believe him. There was no reason for Said to lie. He could not have wanted Pete killed, at least at this stage of the game. But then, the game was none too clear as yet.

"Well, there are other dragomen in Egypt." Said smiled, any grief for Osman well disguised. "But now we have work to do and your days of sightseeing are over."

"They weren't very convincing to begin with," said Pete.

Said looked surprised. "What do you mean?"

"Well, if I was supposed to come up here and pose as a tourist, it was all a big flop, because the one person who shouldn't have known why I was here did know, and as far as I can tell nobody else gives a damn, except him and the law."

"You're referring to Mohammed Ali? Yes? Well, how do you know that he was supposed to be fooled by your masquerade? Have you considered the possibility that he might be one of us?"

Pete nodded. "Sure, and when I mentioned it you told me he would give anything to lay his hands on the necklace."

Said laughed. "You have me there. Let's put it this way: The Inspector is our man on the police. There's little chance of our doing anything without his co operation. In the past he has proved himself to be honest. That is, he lived up to his agreements, helped us smuggle various odds and ends out of the country, and never tried to—what is your nice American expression—hold us up. This time we're not so sure. You see, our other…consignments have been bulky and the machinery of getting them abroad was complex. There was really no way the good Inspector could take our business away from us, or would want to, since we took all the chances and he collected his commission, safely and easily."

"But you think this time he's tempted?"

"Tempted is not the word, Pete. Our friend is out of his mind with greed. That necklace could be any man's fortune and Mohammed Ali knows it. He knows, too, that it is easily smuggled—not like one of the usual consignments, when we are forced to hire an entire ship to take care of our cargo. This particular fortune can be carried in a man's pocket or sewn in his coat. It is so easy, too easy, and the Inspector wants it."

"Are you sure?"

"Wouldn't *you* want it?" The question snapped like a lash across the room.

Pete sat back suddenly in the chair. He tried to grin. "You make it sound awful nice," he said.

"I suspect I do," said Said quietly, and his eyelids dropped like a hawk's over the two strange eyes.

Pete changed the subject quickly. "If it was so important— the necklace, I mean—why did you ever let him find out about it in the first place?"

"It's not that easy." Said played with an ivory box. "You see, the necklace is a famous one. There is no real secret about it. I suppose there are at least a dozen people in Egypt who know I have it, and they would like it, too. The Inspector is one of those. I will not go into past history because it is no concern of ours now—except to say that Mohammed Ali tried, some years ago, to get the necklace away from my predecessor, and failed. I believe he'll try again."

"In spite of his having been already fixed?"

Said nodded. "In spite of that. I had hoped we would be able to get it out of the country quietly, without any trouble from him, without his knowing, but unfortunately he found out. I'm not sure how. We first received warning last week, from Hélène. He had mentioned it to her."

"At a night club in Cairo," said Pete, suddenly remembering his first sight of the Inspector.

"That's right. You were there, too. He spoke, of course, only of his usual fee for allowing us to get it through the customs—a form of blackmail, since in the case of something so small police protection is hardly important...*unless* someone in the police has found out about it."

"As he did." It was beginning to make a little more sense, thought Pete.

"As he did. We had thought all along that it would be wise to entrust it to someone who would not be under suspicion—preferably one with an American passport."

It was always at this point that Pete's suspicions recurred. "The only thing is," he said reasonably, "that I *am* under suspicion by the one person who wants it the most and who has the best chance of getting it, being a policeman."

The blue eye flashed at him sharply. "If you are careful you have nothing to fear."

Pete shrugged. "What's to prevent him from arresting me for walking on the wrong side of the street? Or, even easier, why arrest me at all when he can just march into my room waving a police badge, cut my throat, and take the necklace with him?"

Said looked thoughtfully across the oasis. "We have taken all that into consideration," he said. "We realize the risk is great. I have confidence in you, though." He smiled. "Any

man who can take care of three—it was three?—bandits in
their own region at night is a likely candidate for survival."

Pete finished his Scotch. "Well, it's not that so much. I
don't flatter myself that you people care one way or the
other what happens to me. But it does matter a hell of a lot
to you what happens to the necklace. I think it's sort of funny
that you're willing to hand it over to a marked man."

The Egyptian sighed. "Take our word for it, Pete. We know
what we're doing."

"Even though the Inspector knows I'm to smuggle the
necklace out of Egypt, and you still don't know, in spite of
your big international hookup, whether or not I might be
dumb enough to try to get off with it myself?"

"I'm sure you wouldn't do that." Said was mild. "For one
thing, you wouldn't know how to dispose of it."

"I could sell the ruby you mentioned."

"Possibly. But what a waste! One tenth of the price we
could get, and you will get a tenth of the final sale anyway."

This was it at last. "You on the level?" Pete was finally
interested; he had been waiting for this since Said's hint a
few days before.

"On the level, Pete." Said looked at him gravely. "We can
have no written agreement, but in an undertaking as delicate as this we must all act in good faith with each other or
else lose everything. Were you to double-cross us, we would
lose the necklace for good, even though the organization of
which we are a part would see that you were punished. Were
we to double-cross you, you could make it extremely difficult for us to dispose of the jewels by giving an alarm."

"Unless I were put away." Pete grinned.

Said frowned. "We are not like that. And so, you see, mutual faith is necessary. You are a partner in this. You will be an agent for us and receive an agent's commission in addition to what we've already given you."

"I'm still not so sure about Mohammed Ali," said Pete. "His knowing, I mean. He's got all the cards. This is his country; he's the police. There's nothing he can't do."

"Remember *us*, Pete." Said was cool. "Remember that we have power, too, in Egypt. Power above the police if we need it. Power to remove a police official who crosses us. He will not act openly against you. Don't be afraid of that. He is a careful man, unwilling to offend us."

"But he wants the necklace."

"Yes, he wants it, and you must be careful. Always keep in the open, near people—but avoid public places like Le Couteau Rouge."

Pete was startled. "How did you know about that?"

Said chuckled. "I hear everything, my boy."

They sat in silence for a moment while Pete considered the situation. He had, he realized, no alternative. This was the only chance he had of making enough money to get himself and Anna away from Egypt and back to the States. If the necklace brought as big a price as Said seemed to think it would and if he was actually given a tenth of that price, it would be a tidy amount to settle down with, to start a new life on. It sounded good; it sounded a little too good. "By the way," he asked, "what was the point of my coming here? The Inspector was onto me anyway and—"

"But *I* wasn't," said the Egyptian pleasantly. "I wanted to get to know you first and that was easier up here."

"Then why was it so important for me to trail around after Osman, acting like a tourist? There was nobody to fool, was there?"

Said looked at him a moment without expression; then he said, "There are others interested in our property. You must be discreet."

"Others? Who?"

"Stop seeing that girl." It came out harshly, unexpectedly.

"Anna? But—"

"Take my word for it. Don't see her if you want to get out of this alive." Then, before Pete could protest, could demand an explanation, Said stood up. "Let me show you my cellar," he said easily. "It has the distinction, I believe, of being the only real cellar in Upper Egypt. And it has other distinctions, too, of course."

Mystified, Pete followed him out of the study and into a drawing room, richly furnished with Moorish tapestries upon the wall and a floor of mosaic arranged in exotic patterns. Said pushed open a door hidden by tapestry and Pete followed him down a narrow flight of stone stairs. It was like the tombs, he thought uneasily as he stood behind Said, who was working the combination to the heavy metal door at the foot of the steps. Noiselessly the door opened and Pete followed him into a stone crypt. For a moment they stood in blackness, a hot, airless place; Pete found himself gasping for breath until a gust of air from the open door behind them restored oxygen to his lungs. A light flashed on.

The room was fairly large with a low ceiling. The walls were of stone blocks and the floor was hard-packed sand. Every available bit of space was occupied with mummy cases and ancient relics, chariots, statues inlaid with gold and ivory, boxes of lapis-lazuli scarabs. Over everything hung a strange odor of ancient sandalwood and incense.

"These are my treasures," said the Egyptian, leading Pete between the statues of golden kings seated in ivory chairs. "I collect them for my own amusement. Some are very valuable and I am forced, every now and then, to send one on a long journey to another country." As he talked his hands caressed the statues as though they were alive. It was oddly unpleasant, Pete thought.

At the far end of the crowded room, Said rummaged about among a number of small, highly decorated chests of inlaid wood. The one he wanted, however, was quite small and plain, fashioned of some pale stone with silver hinges.

"Alabaster," murmured Said as he brought the little box into the light and placed it carefully on a stone sarcophagus. Then he opened it and took out the necklace of Queen Tiy.

Even to Pete's untrained eye it was a marvelous work: a collar of bright gold and blue enamel set with dark blue and red stones. But the unusual part was the pendant, which was shaped like the head of a hawk in whose beak was suspended an enormous pear-shaped ruby, as large as a pigeon's egg and gleaming luminous red in the dim light. Pete had never seen anything like it.

Said fondled it for a moment in silence. Then he handed it to Pete. "You must guard it well," he said.

Pete nodded as he felt the cool gold in his hands. The necklace was lighter than it looked, the gold as thin as paper, but firm, unbent after three thousand years. "How will I handle it?" he asked.

"I'll show you." Said led him back upstairs to the study, where he clapped his hands twice. A servant appeared. Said mumbled an order and the servant disappeared while Pete stood awkwardly by the window, holding the necklace in his hands.

A moment later a veiled woman appeared. She made a low bow and stood before them, her eyes on the floor. Said turned to Pete. "Take off your coat," he said. Pete did so and watched with interest as the woman deftly ripped open the lining and placed the necklace inside near the shoulder, where it would not show; in a matter of minutes, she had sewn it in. When she was finished, she left the room as quietly as she had come.

"There." Said smiled, tossing him the coat. "How's that for a good job?"

Pete held up the coat and examined it. The job was extraordinary. The necklace had been placed in the armpit, so that even if someone were to clap him on the shoulder it could not be felt. "Now all I got to remember is to keep my coat on," said Pete, slipping it on.

"Especially when you have a gun in your belt."

Pete flushed; he had forgotten it. "Well, those were orders."

"That's right, those were orders. Well, Pete, I wish you luck. We shall probably not meet again. You will take the train tomorrow to Cairo and there you will contact Hélène, who will give you final instructions. She will make all further arrangements."

"One thing," said Pete, as they walked to the door. "Why did you tell me to stay away from Anna?"

Said paused. They were in the hall. A servant stood ready to open the door. "Ask her one day, if you're foolish enough to keep seeing her, how well she knows Le Mouche. Now, Allah be with you." And they parted.

When he got back to the hotel he found that Anna was out, shopping in the town, but she would be back in time for dinner, according to the manager, that master of misinformation. Idly Pete strolled out into the garden at the back of the hotel. Under the trees was a certain coolness, for which he was grateful. He sat on a bench in the shade and looked west toward the river.

Boats with red sails tacked across the snake-gray water. A flight of birds crossed the blazing sun. For a moment he was at peace, all thought of trouble gone in the warm green silence of the garden. He shut his eyes and dreamed of Anna, of the life they would have together in the States. He saw a house, children in the vague background. But he saw no job, and thinking of that, he opened his eyes again, frowning slightly. Would they really give him a part of the proceeds from the necklace? He could feel the weight of the jewels against his side. They were his if he wanted them, if he had the nerve to double-cross Said and Hélène. He put this out of his mind. There were rules even for those who lived outside the law. He could break the laws of Egypt, of the United

States, but he could not break those laws that demanded
that partners in desperate adventures play it straight with
one another.

But why was he a partner in this scheme? Why had they
asked him to do what they themselves could obviously have
done better? Said's reasons had been good, but not good
enough. He wondered if perhaps they were testing him and,
if so, for what?

Then he remembered what Said had said about Anna
and he grew suddenly cold at the thought. Was it possible
she wanted the necklace? Was it possible that all her words
of love had been false? A means to an end? Even while he
considered this possibility, he knew instinctively that Anna
was his. At the worst, she was being controlled by others.
He thought back over all that she had said and left unsaid
about her situation in Egypt. But no matter how hard he
tried, he could make no real sense of it. She was involved,
some way or other, with the government and the King. She
was not free to do as she pleased and she was also very
likely under the surveillance of the police. The simple
explanation that she was the King's mistress and he was
keeping an eye on her did not explain the apparent freedom
with which she had behaved here in Luxor; then, too, he
believed her when she told him there had been nothing
between her and the King. The mystery of her behavior
was impenetrable. All that he could believe in, finally, was
her love.

Mohammed Ali appeared in the French window of the
dining room and looked about him. Pete wondered whether

or not he should light out, avoiding a meeting with the eager Inspector, but he was spotted before he could hide.

The policeman was as cordial as ever. "Feeling better?" he asked, sitting down uninvited beside Pete.

"I'm all right." Pete moved to the far end of the bench.

"I'm glad. I have been looking for you all afternoon. I supposed you were at Said Pasha's, and of course I didn't want to interrupt your conference."

"You did once before."

"Exactly, and for that reason I shouldn't like to do it again. I have the highest respect for Said Pasha. He is one of the great men of Egypt."

Pete did not bother to ask why Said was great; instead he asked why Mohammed Ali wanted to see him.

"We wished to know if you cared to file a report concerning your—misadventure across the river. If so, I will be happy to make it out for you."

"No report."

"As you wish. They are a nuisance, but the law says they must be made, if the victim wishes."

"Well, the victim doesn't wish any more trouble than he has already."

"You did see Said?" The look Mohammed Ali gave him was sharp as a knife.

"I thought you knew everything I did."

"Almost everything." The Inspector chuckled, became relaxed again. "But that is no business of mine. You are quite right."

"When I get the necklace I'll let you know," said Pete.

"I hope I won't need to be told," said Mohammed Ali pleasantly, and Pete felt the necklace burning under is arm like hot
coals. The garden became for all its green shade, as close
and stifling as a Turkish bath.

"Won't Said let you know?" Pete played innocent. "I sort of
gathered that you were working close with him and Hélène."

"I am, but that doesn't mean that we necessarily operate
in an atmosphere of—what shall I say?—mutual trust. For
some reason, after all our years of doing business together,
they have decided that I might trick them. Don't deny it. I
know. But Said is a suspicious man and I understand quite
well why he should be suspicious. The necklace is of great
value and there are at least a dozen people in Egypt at this
moment who would risk anything to have it."

"And who know that I'm going to be the one who carries
It from Luxor to Cairo?"

Mohammed Ali shrugged. "How much the others suspect
I do not know, though I can guess."

"For somebody who once told me he knew everything
that was going on in Egypt, you seem to be awfully unin-
formed."

"Perhaps." The Inspector was unruffled. "The others
know Said has the necklace. I am not sure how many suspect
your role in all this. How could they know when even you
and I don't know what you are supposed to do?"

"What do you mean by that?"

"Exactly what I say. I have known Said Pasha for many
years. He is perhaps the cleverest man in Egypt. He never

will do what you think he is going to do. I will admit to you frankly that he does many things that not even I know about until they are done. He does one thing with the right hand and, while you watch him, he accomplishes what he wants with the left hand, swiftly, secretly."

For the first time Mohammed Ali had said something that Pete could believe. "I'm sure of that. Even so, why would be bother having me up here all this time, paying me a salary, if he intended to give the necklace to somebody else to carry?"

"Allah knows," said the Inspector with a sigh. "One thing I am certain of: You will never be taken into his confidence, nor will I."

"And this makes us buddies?"

Mohammed Ali smiled. "Not exactly, but we are both involved in his plans. I am his cover in the police. You are his courier. He uses us both in his own way, and there is an excellent chance that we will never know precisely *how* he has used us. He is afraid I will steal the necklace. Don't deny that, Mr. Wells. I know and you know he is disturbed. As a matter of fact, between us, I am flattered. Imagine the remarkable Said Pasha considering *me* as dangerous to his plans! You have no idea how that pleases me."

"I can guess," said Pete, amused by the other's performance.

"I am sure you can." Pete's irony was ignored. "But I am cautious, too. I should not care to cross Said any more than he would care to cross me. We are cellmated."

"You mean stalemated." Pete thought the slip significant.

"Yes, stalemated. I sometimes miss the unusual words in your language. Did I ever tell you that I was educated in the American College at Beirut?"

Pete said that this was news to him and indicated that it was about all the news he was willing to hear from the Inspector, concerning his private life, anyway.

Mohammed Ali did not pursue the subject. "There are times when I feel you dislike me," he said, almost petulantly.

"I don't dislike you. I just don't trust you as far as I can see you."

"And I have tried to be candid with you. It is very discouraging."

"Candid about what?"

"About our situation, yours and mine. We are both being used by Said Pasha. You must admit that that is a bond."

"So?"

"I wish to repeat only what I requested on the occasion of our first meeting in Luxor, in your room: Let me know when Said gives you the necklace."

Pete laughed. "So that you can take it away from me?"

"I would hardly do that. In the first place, I am sure that you will be an intelligent and tough custodian, and in the second place, Said is already suspicious of me and I should not like to make an enemy of him."

"Is he that powerful?"

"He is more powerful than you will ever know, my friend."

"Then what's to keep you from turning me over to the police when you know that I have the jewels?"

Mohammed Ali smiled. "If I did that, Said would have my

head. I anticipate a long and easy life. To cross Said in Egypt would mean the end of ease and probably of life."

Pete was about to remark that the policeman, if he stole the necklace, could probably get out of Egypt altogether and live contentedly on the loot, endangered perhaps by the international organization to which Said claimed to belong but relatively safe if he was clever. Pete pretended, however, to accept this particular line. It was a considerable advantage to have Mohammed Ali believe he was a fool and not on guard.

"I see your point," said Pete slowly. "I don't suppose it will do any harm if you know. I haven't been instructed one way or the other about you. As far as I know, I'm to get the necklace tomorrow and leave for Cairo on the evening train. Then I report to the Countess. Beyond that, I know nothing."

It worked. The Inspector was noticeably relieved, "Good. That is what I thought. Meanwhile, beware of the others."

"What others?"

"Don't you really know?" Mohammed Ali looked at him curiously. "Haven't you suspected?"

"Suspected who?"

"Anna Mueller."

Pete had a sudden inspiration. Could it be that Said and the Inspector were working together? It was too much of a coincidence that both should warn him against Anna in the same way and on the same day. "What makes you think she wants it?"

"Ask her about her friend Le Mouche." And though Pete questioned him further he could get no more out of him.

Anna reappeared at five, flushed from her trip in the hot sun to the town. She had several small packages, which Pete took as she entered the lobby. "I'm worn out," she said as they walked to her room, the manager pretending not to watch them.

When they got to the room, Pete told her that Mohammed Ali was hot on his trail. He didn't explain why and she didn't ask. "We've got to get out of here, baby. To Cairo. Tonight."

"But—well, I mean are you sure it won't be all right to stay over another day?"

He shook his head. "Not if I want to stay alive."

She looked at him seriously for a moment; then: "In that case we must go."

He was suddenly glad. There had been no hesitation. Whatever her plans were, she had been willing to change them for him. "What's the best way of getting to Cairo without that policeman finding out?"

She thought a moment. "Fly, I think."

"Is there a scheduled flight tonight?"

She shook her head. "You can charter a plane. It's not too expensive. Many people do it all the time. It's quick and in this country many places are difficult to reach. I flew here myself. I'll see if I can find the pilot's name." While she looked for it, Pete went to his own room and packed, leaving the Stanley Hotel as a forwarding address. The manager would undoubtedly be upset to have a guest depart without paying his bill, but Pete could take no chances; he didn't want it known he was going.

Anna was talking German over the phone when he returned with his suitcase. After a quick sentence or two, she hung up. "A countryman," she smiled. "The same who flew me here."

"Will he take us?"

She nodded. "He'll be ready at the airport in an hour."

"Good girl." He took her in his arms briefly and kissed her.

He helped her pack and then they slipped over the balcony into the garden of the hotel and, undetected, crossed a grove of trees to the street beyond, where carriages waited. It was not until they were almost to the airport that Pete asked her about Le Mouche.

But all she said was: "I'll tell you when I can, Peter, but not now. Don't ask me now."

Chapter Six

Long before dawn they were circling over the golden lights of the old city, but by the time they got from the airport to the hotel, the moon had set and dawn lingered fresh in the air. To his surprise and pleasure, she agreed to go with him to the Stanley.

Shortly before noon they awakened, ordered coffee in the room, and then, while Anna sat at a dressing table arranging her long hair in the glass, they talked for the first time of why Pete had gone to Luxor, of his criminal mission.

"I think I knew from the beginning," she said thoughtfully. He sat on the bed opposite her, wearing only his trousers, his bare toes making designs on the cool tile floor.

"Well, I thought since we've come this far together, you ought to know the whole thing." He was a little surprised at himself; he had not intended to tell her anything. He had been warned and, as a cautious man, he should have told her no more than he had to. It was to her credit that she had never asked him, even when it had been more than obvious that he was involved in some elaborate game.

"You have it now, this necklace?"

He nodded, but he did not tell her where it was.

"Then turn it over to that woman, Peter." She spoke urgently, looking at his reflection in the mirror.

"What do you mean?"

Get rid of it. Tell her you won't go through with this insane business. Tell her that." She turned and faced him, her face serious. "Peter, you will be killed for that necklace. I know it. I feel it. They are clever and cold, cold as death. They won't give you a chance in the world to live, if only because you know too much about them all. Say you'll refuse to go on with this, please…for my sake." There was no mistaking the sincerity of her appeal; he was glad he had told her at last.

"But I can't, baby. As you say, I already know too much, and on top of that, having gone through so much already for the damned thing, I don't want to lose out on the final sale."

"You *will* lose out anyway, Peter," she said emptily. "It may be too late already."

"Well, if it is, then there's nothing to be done anyway."

She shook her head fiercely. "No, don't say that! We must try to survive. Sometimes it looks hopeless, like a terrible web, but if we are strong enough we can get loose. I am so tired of being helpless, Peter. I am so tired of being pushed this way and that by the killers. And that's what they are, the whole vicious lot of them." And she began to sob. He took her in his arms and they sat side by side for several minutes while she recovered.

When at last she was herself again, she smiled wanly, brushing the tears from her face. "I am very silly," she said. "But there is so much that is so awful, at times I don't think I can stand it another minute. First, Dachau and my father, and then the world after the war, and then this country where

I…where I'm trapped, too, worse even than you. At times I feel as though I were being slowly strangled to death."

"We'll leave, Anna. I can get the rest of the money they owe me, I think, and then we'll have enough to get a ship from Alexandria to Naples. It'll be easy. Then we'll go home and you'll forget all about everything."

But she only sighed. "I was weak. Forget what I said. I have a job to do and so have you. When they are done we can think about leaving. Not until then."

Pete was puzzled. "I thought you said—"

"I wanted you to quit? Yes, I do. I wish for your sake that you would give the necklace to the Rastignac woman, but I am afraid that if you did you would still be as marked as you are now, perhaps more so, because then Said would suspect you of treachery and long before you left Egypt he would have you killed. I know their kind so well. They are the same in every country. I first knew such people in Hamburg after the war, when I went there to sing. I found out soon enough what the world was like—our world in this awful time, at least. They are in control, everywhere. Worse men than Hitler, for he at least had an ideal, terrible as it was. Worse because they have no pity, only hate for the world they mean to own, to steal from the rest of us. And that's why, if I had to lose my life for anything, I should give it gladly if I thought I could kill even one of these monsters as a warning to all the others." She stopped, her face flushed; then she laughed with embarrassment. "I am now making speeches like a politician. Forgive me, Peter."

"I know what you mean." And he did; what she had said with such passion moved him. It was a rare thing, this abstract love for justice that she had, but chilling, too; she was no longer the Anna he had known when she talked like this.

She finished her dressing. They talked more quietly, more practically of his problem. "You must be on your guard every minute, my darling. Especially with the Rastignac woman."

"Jealous?"

She smiled. "Well, yes, now that you mention it. I have seen her once or twice, though we've never met. She is lovely but bad. You know she was the Nazi Raedermann's mistress. Now she is the mistress of Said."

This was news. "How do you know that?"

"I thought everyone knew it. I travel in high circles." She smiled wryly. Pete remembered what he had said to Said about Hélène. What a fool Said must have thought him! He writhed in memory. He was also alarmed. If Said thought he was interested in Hélène and that Hélène might return that interest, it could complicate a tangled situation even more, might tangle it fatally.

"I wish you'd told me that earlier."

Anna was amused. "You mean that she was my—predecessor in your affections?"

"Not even close," he said grimly. "But I made a crack or two to Said about her. I hope he didn't resent it."

"He won't if he needs you. They put their personal affairs second. I am quite sure that she conducts any number of seductions at his suggestion. But watch out for her. Mohammed Ali is far less likely to be dangerous."

"But what about you?"

"Me?" She looked startled.

"The business you're involved in—what about that? Can't you tell me now what it is? Why you can't leave Egypt?"

She shook her head. "If it was only for my own sake I would tell you, I would trust you. But others are involved. I can't betray them."

"When will you be able to tell me?"

"Soon, I hope, very soon. Then we can go." But there was a deadness in her voice that bothered him, as though she knew there would be no life for them together in the future. He started to say something, to try to jolt the truth from her before it was too late, but the misery in her dark blue eyes stopped him. He did not speak.

They left the hotel together. Outside in the street, with still too many things unsaid, they parted. "I'll see you tonight," said Anna, getting into a taxi. "After dinner, late. Don't wait up." She waved to him as she drove off. Disaster was in the air. He turned toward Shepheard's.

Hastings was in the bar when he arrived, as though by prearrangement. His surprise, however, seemed genuine.

"Wells! Good to see you, boy! By God, it is!" He pumped his hand energetically and pulled him over to the bar. "Seen Hélène yet?"

"No, I just got here. I thought I'd look in the bar first, before I called her."

"Spot of gin? Perfect for breakfast, cauterizes the stomach." He ordered two gins and tonic. Then Hastings looked curiously at Pete, his hard pale eyes interested, his lips set in a genial smile. "Didn't expect you till tonight, you know. How'd you get here, by the way?"

"Some people I knew chartered a plane last night. Thought I'd go along, since there was no reason to stay on in Luxor."

"Said know you were leaving?"

"Certainly. He gave me the—"

"Did he know you were leaving last night instead of today?"

The point seemed a little too fine to Pete. "Well, no, I don't suppose he did. Does it matter? He'd already given me the—stuff."

"Doesn't matter at all. Ah, the libation!" They toasted one another solemnly. "By the way," said Hastings, smacking his lips over the gin, "word comes that you are now the Don Juan of Upper Egypt."

Pete chuckled. "There didn't seem any competition," he said.

"Think not?" Hastings was bland. "No competition there, perhaps. But here, ah, watch out."

"Why?"

"When competition wears a crown, it's not easy for us ordinary fellows."

"I don't think it's true about Anna and him."

"That what she told you? Well, it's none of my affair except where it involves us, and it will involve us if you're suddenly marched out of Egypt by the police. That's happened a couple of times before to eager youths, at least to those with foreign passports. Local swains disappear or else become eunuchs."

That was it, at last. "You know?"

Hastings looked at him curiously. "Know what?"

"About what happened to me the other night, on the west side of the river." Pete told the story quickly, aware that Hastings already knew the details.

"We heard," said Hastings, when he finished. "Not all, though. Shocked, too. Mainly by your bad judgment, if you'll excuse my saying so. You, and we, are in a tough situation. Delicacy is all-important. So what do you do? Get tangled up with a girl who is guarded by the police and the main interest of the King. You're damned lucky to be here at all."

Pete was irritated, partly because what Hastings said had some truth in it—he had acted foolishly. On the other hand, Anna was more important to him than business, than his own safety. "If you want," said Pete recklessly, "you can take the necklace and—"

"Keep your voice down, boy," said Hastings with a cool smile, his eyes like ice. A group of Egyptians had entered the bar and sat down at a table nearby. He lowered his own voice carefully. "Now don't fly off the handle. Thought you were a clever chap, lot of nerve, control, that kind of thing. And here you are acting like a schoolboy. Surprised at you."

"I just think my private life is no concern of yours," said Pete in a low voice, aware that, in a sense, he was wrong.

"As far as I'm concerned, you can go live with that police-man on a houseboat," said Hastings, suddenly lyric. "I don't care. But don't get involved until you're clear, until we're all clear. You've got in trouble once already. Suppose you'd had the necklace with you then? Been merry hell to pay for the lot of us."

Pete mumbled that he was sorry. "Well, you won't have much longer," said Hastings cheerily.

"How much longer, do you think?"

"A day or two."

"And then I leave the country with the necklace?"

"Can't tell just yet. Hélène's making those plans now. Depends a lot on the situation."

"Why? Is there any trouble? Are the police—"

"Never worry about the police in an Arab country. They don't cost much, and when they're bought they usually stay bought, though of course that's no sure sign Mohammed Ali may not be ambitious. No, the police won't bother us. Others will. Another...syndicate is after the necklace. Even so, you're fairly safe, if all goes well, and by that I mean politics."

Pete was puzzled.

"Politics," repeated Hastings, and his voice descended almost to a whisper. "There are rumors of a plot against the King. Trouble, real trouble. Nobody knows what might happen. If there's out-and-out rioting it may be difficult to follow any schedule."

"Then why not let me leave now, today? I can take a plane and be off in a few hours."

Hastings chuckled. "I like that. Eager. Wonderful quality. Unfortunately, we have a schedule. Certain people must be alerted; others thrown off the scent. Your coming here unexpectedly probably shook some of them loose; they'll be a while getting on to you again."

"You mean others, people I don't know about, are following me around, trying to get the stuff?"

"Certainly, my boy. Not nervous, are you?"

Pete swallowed part of his gin the wrong way; he coughed for several moments while Hastings pounded his back. "Didn't mean to upset you." Hastings chuckled. "Well, come along. Let's find Hélène."

She was free for lunch. Hastings called her on the house phone and a few minutes later, dazzling in a batik dress, she joined them out on the terrace in back of the hotel, where, under an awning overlooking the garden, lunch was served.

"We did not expect you so soon." She smiled warmly and put her hand on his sleeve as though seeing him at last made up for everything, even the unexpectedness of his arrival.

"It was too hot in Luxor."

"Meaning the weather?" asked Hastings.

Pete laughed. "That was too hot, too. No, it was getting uncomfortable with Mohammed Ali around all the time. I couldn't wait to duck him. When Said gave me the necklace I figured I was free to go right then. I never thought there was a special reason for me to wait another day, especially with him hot on my trail."

"You did exactly right," said Hélène, somewhat to his surprise. "You must run no more risks than you have to."

"In that case, I wish you'd hold onto the necklace until it's time for me to skip the country with it. I can't sleep nights knowing that there's a hundred thousand bucks or so tucked away in my coat."

"Lobster, I think," said Hastings to the waiter, speaking for all of them. "Marvelous lobsters in these parts."

Hélène ignored Hastings. "I can't do that," she said. "It wouldn't work."

"I don't see why not. This is your city. You must have all sorts of good hiding places. I think you'd want it kept in a safe place. They can get me almost any day. There's not a hell of a lot one man can do in a strange city against a dozen sharp customers who want something he's got."

"Lad who can take care of three bandits shouldn't be frightened of some nervous jewel thieves." Hastings poured wine with an accurate hand.

"I know what he means," said Hélène hesitantly. "It has bothered me also. Peter, we can't take the necklace now because we are watched, too, even at this minute. More important, though, we have no idea yet when you are to go. It depends on Said. On the situation here. On the negotiations with our buyer, which Said himself is conducting. For all I know, he may suddenly call us now, this minute, and send you to Europe."

"Then the decision is his, finally?"

Hélène nodded. "Entirely his. Our only job is to make the arrangements. It will be best, probably, for you to fly, but all will depend on how much warning we have."

"So meanwhile I wander about the city with a small fortune in my coat, which I don't dare take off even when I go to sleep, and your whole scheme depends on my keeping out of the hands of police and competitors." He sighed. "You have a lot of faith, I'll say that."

"We do, Peter. Don't you understand there isn't anything else we can do right now? Now that you know our situation a little better, you can see that it is like an army, in a way. We must follow orders, all of us. Our orders are to get you out of the country at a moment's notice when the deal in Europe or America is completed. Your orders are to stand by, with the necklace, until we give the word."

He had to admit to himself that she was plausible, but a suspicion had begun to grow, an ugly indication of a plot so intricate that it made his head spin. Until he was sure, however, he would pretend ignorance. "Whatever you say. It's almost as much your worry as mine. You'll lose a fortune and I'll get my throat cut."

"I think we should have champagne. Just the stuff for a day like this. Celebrate a bit. Lunch's best time for it, I always say." And Hastings ordered champagne, which they drank thirstily, enjoying its coolness in the hot afternoon.

After lunch Hastings, as usual, excused himself, leaving Pete to Hélène, who had obviously been selected as the one who could best handle the young American.

"I suppose you'll be glad when it's over," she said, as they sat back in their canvas chairs while the waiter cleared the table.

He nodded. "Real glad," he said.

"I should never have asked you to take on this job," She looked at him with concern. "The danger is greater than the reward, though it is certainly not to my interest to tell you this." She gave every appearance of trying to be honest.

"Meaning I won't get that percentage I was promised?"

"Meaning that even when you do get it you will not be sufficiently compensated for all you've done for us. You are very

brave, Peter." She turned her dark eyes on him, and the
expression was warm and candid. Under the table her leg
pressed gently, unmistakably against his. A spasm of desire
went through him for an instant, but only for an instant.
There was no other woman for him now but Anna. Deliberately, cold-bloodedly, he returned the pressure, noting with
a scientist's detachment the faint flush of color that rose from
her neck to her face.

"I missed you," she said softly, looking away.

"I thought about you, too," he said.

She looked back at him slyly. "Not too much. I have heard
about the German girl."

"That didn't mean anything," he said. He let his fingers
run over her bare arm. The soft skin was like a shock. It
would be different from Anna, he thought grimly, if it happened. Judging from Helene's past performance, she would
tease a lot, but at the last minute she would avoid following
through. It was possible that he had a surprise or two in
store for her.

"Where will you go when you leave Egypt?" she asked,
sitting very straight beside him while his strong rough fingers
caressed her arm.

"If I leave here."

"You mean you might stay?"

"Why not? Six feet under is as good here as anywhere.
Maybe better. The sand keeps the body in good shape."

She shuddered. "Don't say that. You won't be killed. There
is a difference between danger and—and that. People are not

so easily killed in a city like Cairo, certainly not Americans. Your passport is like armor."

"It didn't help much the night I was mugged in the tombs."

"You were foolish. That was a bad place. No, if you keep a careful lookout, avoid dark empty places, you will be all right. I promise you that, *chéri.*"

He hid his mistrust of her. "I'll do what you say." He grinned suddenly. "I'm a bit short of cash. I was wondering if…"

"Of course. We'll pay you the other hundred pounds now, if you like. Do you want English or Egyptian currency?"

He said he preferred American, but he'd settle for English.

"Do you want to come with me while I get it?" She looked him full in the face, a half-smile on her lips. He had a brief malevolent desire to shatter this cool mocking woman's mask, to find what was underneath.

He followed her then to her room, where she rummaged through her dressing table until she found a black leather jewel box, in which, among diamonds, she kept a wad of currency. She counted out a hundred pounds, appearing not to be aware of him, standing behind her, so close that he could almost hear the rapid beating of her heart. She turned. They were now so close that they almost touched. He stepped back, with a great effort of will. This was not the time, not yet. She looked at him, surprised; she had expected some sort of advance and none had come. He took the money.

"Thanks a lot. I'll need it." They stood awkwardly for a moment. He was pleased to see her ill at ease.

Finally she said, "You seem different, *chéri*. Has something happened?" She lit a cigarette and this bit of business relaxed her, gave her an excuse to move away from him to the armchair by the window, where she sat down. He sat opposite her, on a straight chair.

"I don't know what you mean."

"Oh, I think you do." She was gradually regaining control. "When you left you were… Well, there was more fire. I felt that we had a kind of understanding. Now something's happened. You love her, don't you?" This was abrupt.

He smiled, wondering what to say. "She's a nice girl," he said at last, trying to be offhand.

"But not for you. She is not free, in any sense."

"You mean because of the King?"

"Partly, yes. Though not in the way you might think. She is watched day and night, and that is bad for you, for us. We are in sufficient danger as it is without having you become involved with Anna Mueller."

"Why? What's all the mystery about? What's she done, besides go out with the local boss a few times?"

Hélène smiled. "What a funny way to speak of the King! But you're right, he is the local boss, and he is the law, as you'll find out if you try to cross him or any of his henchmen."

"We'll see," said Pete, sounding more brave than he felt. It would be his luck to fall for the one girl in the country who was the most dangerous to know. Well, it couldn't be helped. "Oh," he said, changing the subject, "I saw a picture of you in Said's house, with that Nazi. What's his name, Raedermann?"

She took this very well; her face did not change expression. "Yes, we were good friends. I told you I was an agent."

"For the Free French."

"So I was. I knew many people, many Nazis, Communists, all sorts of people. We were like freemasons, the agents in those days."

"They tell me you were pretty free," said Pete, not intending this to sound as insulting as it did.

She flushed angrily. "I suggest it is none of your business."

"I'm sorry. I didn't mean it like that. I mean Free French. Only it seemed funny that you were able to be such good friends with a Nazi big shot. That's all I meant."

She had recovered her poise by then. "Well, those were confused times, *chéri*, far more so than now. We were none of us too sure where our loyalties lay. But let's not talk about such unpleasant things. Erich is dead, that war is over, the next one hasn't begun, and you are soon to make money for us and yourself. What could be nicer?"

Pete agreed that it was pretty nice. There was another silence, and this time the tension between them was great, like an electric current in the warm air. But then, just before it became unbearable, he stood up and said, "I've got to go to the Consulate and see about those traveler's checks I lost."

Surprise and irritation crossed her face like the shadow of a cloud. Her voice did not betray her, though. "I'm sorry." She rose, too. "Perhaps it's better, *chéri*, that we see only a little of each other. Avoid the girl, though, until our business is complete. After that do as you must. Will you keep in touch with me here, twice a day? Telephone in the morning and later in the day, before dinner. We should have word from Said soon." She walked with him to the door.

Without shaking hands, avoiding physical contact of any kind, he left her, pleased with his own will and, more important, pleased that he had made her think him a fool. He had kept his suspicions to himself. He was not yet sure of the dimensions of the plot, but he knew that the danger he faced came as much from Hélène and Said as it did from Mohammed Ali. He knew instinctively that he was intended to be a victim. He also knew that, if he was, they would suffer, too. He set his jaw coldly. Time was running out.

Mr. Case seemed surprised to see him when he entered his office at the Consulate.

"We were beginning to wonder what had happened to you, Mr. Walsh—I mean Wells. Sit down." He sounded almost cordial. "There've been a number of inquiries about you."

"That right? Who from?"

"I'm afraid I'm not at liberty to say. Only this morning, though, the Consul General asked me about you." This fact seemed to impress Mr. Case.

"I hope to hell he did. I'd still like to know what happened to my traveler's checks."

Mr. Case frowned. "Ah, those. I'm afraid you'll have to write them off. We found one in Alexandria that had been cashed by a moneylender. That means they are in the hands of a thief who knows what he is doing. I expect they have all been cashed by now. We wrote New Orleans, but so far no answer. You were in Luxor, weren't you?"

"That's right, seeing the sights."

"You must be in business, then." Mr. Case smiled politely. "I was under the impression you had no money the other day when you were in here."

"Well, I'll tell you. A good fairy came and put it under my pillow."

"I was merely inquiring," said Mr. Case, growing red. "I must tell you, though, that it would be a very good idea for you to leave the country, if you can."

"Leave? I just got here."

"I have no idea, Mr. Wells, what you are up to, but there is every indication that a first-class incident is in the making, and the Consulate feels that you, as an American citizen, should avoid making any trouble for yourself or for our government."

"I don't follow you."

"Then I won't lead you," snapped Mr. Case. "The Consul General told me to tell you this if you came in here. We can only advise. You're welcome to take it or leave it."

"What kind of incident?"

"Political. This country is about to blow up. All Americans have been asked to leave or else move out into the suburbs. Since you, in particular, have seen fit to get mixed up with the local…businessmen, I think you would be doing both yourself and us a favor if you left Egypt by the next plane. I assume you have enough money. If not, it is just possible that we…"

"That's sure white of you. When I needed help you wouldn't give me a cent; now that I look like a possible embarrassment, nothing's too good for me." Pete was a little bitter; the trick was so obvious. He wondered what it was the Consul had heard.

"I'm sorry you take it that way, Mr. Wells. But our first interest is the United States, not you."

"That's fair." Pete rose. "I suppose you'll tell me now to keep out of sight, to watch out."

"As a matter of fact, I was going to suggest exactly that. We've given the same advice to all Americans. If this mob should start making trouble, anyone wearing Western clothes, whether Egyptian or American or European, will be torn to pieces. I have also been instructed to tell all nationals that should there be rioting in the streets, they are free to come to the Consulate here for protection."

"Can you tell me anything about a man named Hastings or a woman named De Rastignac?"

Mr. Case shook his head as though he had never heard of either.

"What do you know about Anna Mueller?"

This had an effect. "Only what I hear in Cairo, what everybody hears."

"That she and the King…"

"Exactly," interrupted the official nervously, as though afraid of being overheard. "Now, if you should change your mind about leaving Cairo, and we hope you will, please feel free…" But Pete was gone before the sentence had been finished.

He walked back to the Stanley.

If anything unusual was going on in the city, he couldn't spot it. Everything seemed perfectly ordinary. The beggars were everywhere, loud as ever. Street vendors shouted their wares in high monotonous voices. The expensive modern cars honked their horns and shifted gears smoothly in the broad main streets. Only the presence of more policemen than usual in front of certain buildings suggested that there was trouble brewing.

Back at the Stanley, he found two messages for him, which he crumpled in his pocket as he went upstairs to his room.

He knew the contents of one of the notes before he read it: Anna had gone. Her suitcases were missing and there was no trace in the room that she had ever been there. He tore open the two envelopes. One contained the bill for his room at the Karnak Inn, with a polite note from the manager. The other was from Anna.

He sat down shakily on the bed and read: "My darling, things are happening so quickly now that I hardly know what to tell you or what to do. I couldn't stay with you at the hotel because, for your own sake, it would be bad. The one thing that I must do must be done now and I no longer have any choice. Don't try to find me, please. You must trust me and if there is any chance of our being together afterward I will come back, I promise. Believe me when I say I love you. Your own Anna." That was all there was to it. He sat, stunned, holding the letter in his hands, the last link he had with her, the only sign that she had ever lived and he had known her.

The telephone rang; dumbly he answered it.

"I'm glad to find you home, Mr. Wells. May I come up? I'm in the lobby." Pete grunted and put the phone back on its hook. Nothing made any difference now until he found Anna. He awaited his visitor without interest.

Mohammed Ali was in uniform, wearing a pistol holster. He smiled when he saw Pete and shook his hand warmly "You left so suddenly, my friend. We were all afraid something might have happened to you."

"But the manager remembered to tell you that I was back at the Stanley."

"So he did. Where is Fräulein Mueller? We were given to understand that she was with you here."

"Your news isn't up to date. She's taken a trip."

"I see. Perhaps it is all for the best. Fortunately, no harm can come to her."

"What makes you so sure?"

"Haven't you guessed? Because of her important friend she is always guarded, always watched by the police."

"Then how come you have no idea where she is?"

"I am no longer her guardian," said Mohammed Ali smoothly, sitting carefully on the edge of a small table. "I could probably find out by calling headquarters."

"Why don't you?"

"Because I'm not interested."

"Well, I am."

"Would you care to make a bargain?" The policeman was looking at him intently now, his eyes glittering beneath dark brows.

"What kind of bargain?" The expression on the Arab's face was answer enough. "No, none of that, Junior. That's asking too much."

"But suppose she is in danger, wouldn't you like to know that?"

"You said yourself that it was the job of you guys to keep her out of trouble, to protect her."

"Why do you hate me?" Mohammed Ali was pale and tense. "Do I disgust you so? I can save you. I am the only person in Egypt who can. If I want to I can keep them from killing you, and they will kill you—soon, very soon."

"Who will?"

But the policeman only shook his head, his eyes glittering as he studied Pete.

Casually Pete swung one leg over the bed. "Maybe they'll change their minds," he said; then he grinned. "I wonder just how friendly you were feeling on the train when you had that bug planted on me."

"For your own good, believe me," said Mohammed Ali intensely. "You would have been ill for a week, by which time the affair would have been out of your hands."

"I'm glad you have my interest at heart." Pete mocked him, coldly gauging to himself the distance between them, calculating a defense.

"I have," said the Inspector in a strange low voice. "Let me show you." He moved toward Pete, who jumped quickly from the bed, doubling his fists and crouching all in one quick movement. The policeman stepped back. "Then it is all over for you," said Mohammed Ali flatly. "This was your chance. If you had …"

"Being dead doesn't seem so unattractive. Now get out."

The policeman shook his head. "Not until you give me the necklace."

Pete's fingers twitched nervously at his belt, ready to grab his revolver. "I haven't got it," he said. "I gave it to Hélène this morning.

"No, you still have it," said the policeman quietly. "I want it." He drew his gun. Pete made no move yet; he was thinking quickly.

"I tell you, I gave it to her. You can search me if you want to. She's supposed to hang onto it until Said gives the word for me to take it out of the country."

"Give it to me or I'll shoot," said the Inspector, and with a click he released the safety catch.

"No, you won't," said Pete, with great effort keeping his voice steady though his throat had suddenly gone dry and his tongue threatened to stick to the roof of his mouth. He was able to speak quietly, though. "They know downstairs that you came up here. If you shoot an American citizen there'll be an investigation and they'll know you were the one who did it."

"I am the police. Give me that necklace."

"If you take it, if you kill me, Said will find out, and that'll be the end of you, even if you try to leave the country. He's part of an international organization. You know what that means, don't you? I guess you do. Maybe you're part of it too. Well, cross them up…" He spoke fast and he knew that he was making a little headway, for the policeman's aim wavered.

"Give it to me," he said.

"Hell, man, I told you I don't have it! Here, come on, search me. I swear I don't have it. You don't have to kill me to find out." Pete put his arms high up over his head. Mohammed Ali approached, pressing the muzzle of the revolver into Pete's belly. With his other hand he undid the coat and slipped his hand inside, both searching and caressing. Pete flushed. "I'm ticklish," he said, but the Inspector continued his search. Then, just as his hand moved upward on the right side, near the armpit, near the necklace, Pete brought both hands down with a crash on the back of the Arab's neck.

The revolver clattered to the floor. Mohammed Ali grunted and fell forward, knocking Pete off balance. They both fell against the bed and rolled onto the floor, Mohammed Ali on top.

The fight took a long time, or so it seemed to Pete. On his feet he could have taken care of the larger man in a few seconds, but at close quarters, wrestling, he was handicapped by the other's weight and brute strength.

They fought silently, only an occasional gasp when one hurt the other. Neither wanted the fight interrupted by strangers. They rolled across the floor, Pete trying to get to his feet, the other holding him back deliberately, aware of the American's powerful fists.

Pete saw his tactics in a flash and he fought with even greater ferocity. The Arab was trying to choke him. Each chance he got, the huge hard hands would go to Pete's throat and begin to squeeze; each time Pete got away, kicking, elbowing, shoving.

There were no rules now. Two animals were fighting for survival. Pete tasted blood on his lip, his own blood. His mouth had been cut by his own teeth. The larger man's face was purple and the veins were corded in it like dark ropes, throbbing with strain.

Not until they got beneath the window in their agonizing struggle across the floor did Pete get his first opening. The Arab was growing tired. He relaxed his pressure imperceptibly on Pete's throat, and that was all he needed. With a huge effort he broke away, kicking the Arab in the chest.

Mohammed staggered against the wall, choking. Pete moved in for the kill. It took only two blows, the strong right and the quick left follow-up. The Inspector crumpled, unconscious.

Pete stood in the center of the room, head bowed, arms at his sides, struggling for breath. Blood roared in his ears. Half blind with sweat and fatigue, he plunged his head into the washbasin and turned on the cold water full blast.

It took several minutes for him to recover. When he did, he dried his face and neck and looked in the mirror. His mouth was not badly cut, but the upper lip was beginning to swell. The cold water had stopped the bleeding. His shirt was torn, but his suit, though shapeless, was not damaged.

Quickly, keeping his eye on Mohammed Ali, he changed his shirt, combed his hair, arranged his jacket as well as he could, and then, after first dropping the policeman's revolver behind the pillows on his bed, he left the room, locking the door behind him.

He half expected to see more policemen in the corridor, but there were none about. As casually as possible he walked down the stairs, through the lobby, and out into the street.

He was about to catch a cab when a hand was placed on his shoulder. He gave a start and whirled about, expecting the worst.

But it was only the manager, the plump cockney. "I wouldn't go out there, sir, if I was you."

"Out where?"

"In them streets, sir. There's trouble on its way and I wouldn't like to see nothing 'appen to a chap like you."

"Why? What's up?"

"The mob. They're yelling downtown, we hear. They're in a mean mood and when they are, watch your step."

"I'll do that. Thanks."

"Keep to the main streets, where the police are."

Pete smiled to himself at that. He assured the little man he would be all right. Then he hailed a cab.

Le Couteau Rouge was crowded, considering the earliness of the hour. Pete went straight to the bar and ordered Pernod. While he stood there he looked warily about the room for signs of danger, but no one paid much attention to him. People were too intent on their own problems. Men sat at tables, their heads close together, talking rapidly, fiercely to one another. It was twenty minutes before Pete realized that there were no women in the bar. A strange sign, a sign of trouble. The air was charged with tension.

"Remember me?" Pete asked the bartender with the great mustache.

"*Certainement!* The young *Américain* who loses his money. You find it, *hein*?" Though the man's tone was friendly he seemed distracted, his eyes turning furtively toward the door, as though he expected hostile visitors

"No, never got it back, but I've been working."

"Good, good. I'm glad. You like Luxor? Interesting for the history. You should maybe stay there." The bartender's eyes fixed on Pete's for a moment. He was pale, and he kept polishing and repolishing a clean glass with the end of his apron.

"Why? The town going to blow up?"

"I think maybe, yes." From faraway came the unmistakable sounds of rifles: one volley, then an answering volley, then scattered fire. The whole room became silent. Men turned with frightened faces toward the door. *"Mon Dieu!"* muttered the bartender, and he dropped the glass onto the floor, where it broke. The familiar sound of breaking glass recalled the others. They began to talk again, a low buzzing like a hive of bees. The firing had stopped.

Pete swallowed his Pernod. The liquor burned his upper lip. "Where's Le Mouche?" he asked.

"Là-bas." The bartender motioned with his head toward the back room. "But no one can see him. No one. Monsieur!" But Pete was already halfway to the double door. No one tried to stop him.

He was not surprised when he stepped into the dim corridor to find the door to Le Mouche's room suddenly open, revealing the hunchback standing on the threshold, smiling.

"Come in, my friend, come in. These are difficult times for honest men." He chuckled loudly as Pete followed him into the room.

It was much the same as before, except that the teapot was no longer boiling, and where the hot plate had been on the table there was now a telephone. Le Mouche sat down in his armchair and motioned Pete to sit beside him.

"We have had many experiences, haven't we?" said Le Mouche with a gentle smile, turning his fine dark eyes on Pete.

Pete was not quite sure what he meant. There was too little time, though, to find out, to engage in subtleties. "Where is Anna?"

The hunchback sighed. "I knew you would ask me that. When I saw you come in the bar just now I knew that that was why you were here."

"Do you know?"

Le Mouche nodded. "I know, but I will not tell you. That is her wish and it is also my desire, so please, for the sake of good feeling, don't ask me."

"Good feeling!" Pete exploded. "There isn't such a thing in this whole damned city. The girl I want, the only person I care about, is gone, and I don't know what she's doing or where she is and you tell me I'm not to ask!"

Le Mouche touched his arm gently, affectionately. "It is not so entirely bad, my son." He laughed softly. "I *am* old enough to be your father, you know." He paused for a moment, frowning, as though he had thought of something from the past, some dark memory. Then he said more lightly, "Tomorrow you will be able to see her, if nothing goes wrong. She loves you, you know. There's no doubt of that."

"She's got a fine way of showing it," said Pete bitterly, and he began to shake, a delayed reaction from the fight. "Too—too much adrenalin," he stammered, aware that the hunchback was watching him.

Le Mouche pressed a button beside his chair and the bartender appeared and was told to bring brandy. When Pete drank it he felt better, but weak. All the strength had gone out of him, used up in the fight. It was several minutes before he felt like himself again.

"It will be all right," said Le Mouche quietly. "It will be all right." His voice was low, hypnotic, as he repeated soothing words. Then, when he saw that Pete had recovered, he said, "Try to understand that Anna is not free to do what she wants to do. She has obligations to others, to many others, to people living and even"—he paused—"to people dead. When she has fulfilled them she will be free again, perhaps for the first time."

"She may be dead by then."

"It's possible." Le Mouche looked away. "I hope not. I can tell you nothing more."

"But I just can't sit and wait!" Pete exploded. "Why can't I help her? Why—"

The ringing of the telephone stopped his tirade. Le Mouche spoke Arabic rapidly into the receiver; he was thoughtful as he replaced it. "It is beginning," he said finally, his fingers drumming on the table.

"What's beginning?"

"Revolution, my friend. Solemn word, dangerous word."

"Are you mixed up in it?"

"Everyone is mixed up in it," said Le Mouche evasively. "Now we must ride out the storm. That was a friend of mine with word that rioting has started in El Minzah suburb, a working-class district. That means it will spread very soon to the center of the city."

"What's going on?"

"According to the newspapers, the wicked Jews are trying to overthrow the government because of the situation in Israel. The government always blames it on the Jews. Actually the troubles are almost always spontaneous. Even Moslems will oppose tyrants. The hatred of the King has been building a long time. When it reaches the Army, then—*pfft*, no more King."

"Has it reached the Army yet?"

"We shall know soon enough."

"And you and Anna are mixed up in all this?"

"I never said that."

"But it's what you mean, isn't it?"

"Tomorrow you'll know."

"If we're still alive."

"If not," and Le Mouche smiled, "we'll know more important things. Accept the situation. There is never any use in struggling against events when they have got out of one's personal control, and today, tonight, tomorrow belong to the mob, not to us."

Pete groaned with frustration. "What do you think I ought to do, then?"

"I would advise going immediately to the American Consulate and staying there until the business is over. Then come back here and join Anna. She will be here, in this room, tomorrow."

"If."

"If." From far away they could hear the muffled sound of gunfire. They listened for some minutes until it stopped and the buzz of talk from the adjoining bar began again.

"Now," said Le Mouche, as though nothing had happened, "tell me about your adventures in Luxor."

"Not much to tell. I was sent up there by Hélène, as you probably know, since you seem to know everything else. I met someone called Said, with whom I did business, as agreed. I got into trouble with a police inspector named Mohammed Ali and I met Anna. It was pretty eventful."

"I should think so. You recall, perhaps, that I advised you against having anything to do with Hélène and the others?"

"There wasn't much choice. I didn't have any illusion about them, but I had to make some money, even though they'll cut my throat if it fits their plans, if I let them."

"No, that was not their plan exactly. Mohammed Ali is supposed to do the throat-cutting."

Pete was startled. He wondered if he had heard correctly. "You mean…"

"Give me that necklace, Pete." Le Mouche's voice was stern.

"Oh, no! No, you don't!" Pete jumped to his feet, pulling his gun at the same time and aiming at Le Mouche. "I should have figured you weren't on the level. It was too damned much to expect in this hellhole. You—"

The two men who had come in behind him disarmed him

quickly and, before he could even regain his balance, pushed him back into the chair. Le Mouche smiled sadly. "It looks as though the whole world is against you, I know," he said as Pete struggled helplessly. The two Arabs were enormous men, dressed in the flowing robes of the desert. They held him to the chair with apparently little effort. Le Mouche took his gun and then expertly ripped the lining of his jacket and extracted the necklace.

"Now, if you promise not to move, I'll order them away."

"What the hell good's a promise?" Pete was breathing helplessly, heavily. He almost wished they would finish the job and let him die.

"All I ask is that you listen to me," said Le Mouche reasonably. He motioned with his hand and the two Arabs withdrew, closing the door softly behind them. "They are my guards," explained Le Mouche, almost apologetically, his hand on the butt of Pete's revolver, aware that the young American was prepared to make a break for it.

"I've already had one fight today for that thing," said Pete. "I thought that would be par for the course."

"You won't have to fight for it again," said Le Mouche. Then, to Pete's amazement, he took the necklace and broke it. Beads scattered over the room. The ruby, broken from its pendant, fell to the floor, and Le Mouche ground it with his heel until it broke.

"My God, man!" Pete jumped to his feet excitedly. "That's a fortune! You've just lost us all more money than—" He stopped abruptly, conscious that Le Mouche was laughing at him. "What's the big idea?"

"The idea is not so very big, young man," said the hunch-back, pushing Pete's revolver across the table to him. "I'm sorry I had to take it away from you like that, but I knew you'd never give it up, no matter what I said."

Pete took the gun and shoved it back in his belt. This, he decided, was the end. He slumped in his chair wearily, pre-pared for anything.

"Don't look so tragic." Le Mouche chuckled. "I've just saved you from a great deal of annoyance."

"Not to mention money."

"Don't be bitter. It was only worth about twenty dollars."

"You're out of your mind. That necklace was worth over a hundred grand. The ruby alone was worth—"

"The original, yes. But you've been guarding with your life an imitation, a copy, a fake." It took a moment for this to sink in. Pete tried to speak but there were no words ready on his tongue. Le Mouche explained: "In a way, much of what happened to you is my fault and I can apologize only by get-ting you out of it all now—my fault not so much for what I did as for what I didn't do. I could have stopped you that afternoon when you came here, before you went to Luxor. I liked you. I didn't want you to come to harm, but unfortu-nately, for reasons that you may one day understand, I wasn't free to do more than I did: to warn you not to trust Hélène and Hastings. I could, I suppose, have told you why, but I was not in a position to make trouble for myself, and it would have been grave trouble, then." He paused. The distant boom of light artillery invaded the stillness of the room. Both waited until it had passed.

Le Mouche continued. "Now it matters less. Said, whom I have known for many years, stole the necklace of Queen Tiy some time ago from a wealthy eccentric living at Aswân. I have no doubt he told you a different story, but it was a case of pure thievery and nothing more. He is one of the more efficient crooks in a country distinguished for crime. For some reason he has taken his time about disposing of the necklace. I am told, by others as well as by him, that he has a very real love of antiquities, almost as great a passion as the one he has for money. In any event, it became widely known in our underworld (which is almost the same thing as the everyday world of Cairo) that he had the necklace and that sooner or later he would smuggle it out of the country. A few months ago, he decided the time was ripe to make his sale. He instructed his partners, Hélène and Hastings, to send it by usual consignment to Europe."

"What's usual consignment?"

"By sea. Their trade is the usual narcotics, and on a grand scale. They operate three small ships, and their connections arc worldwide. But, unfortunately for Said, his police contact, the greedy Mohammed Ali, discovered that the necklace was to make its long anticipated voyage to parts unknown, and he hinted—broadly, I gather—that for his co-operation a hefty slice of the proceeds would be in order. That, my friend, is where the innocent young American enters the picture. It was decided that you be used as a decoy. Hélène would send you to Luxor for conferences with Said, which Mohammed Ali undoubtedly would hear of, and then, when he had risen to the bait, you would be given a copy of the necklace and sent back to Cairo, where Mohammed Ali would probably relieve you of the necklace. By returning early, however, you threw the timetable off and doubtless saved your life. You see, Hélène and Said could not feel safe until they were fairly certain that Mohammed Ali had got the imitation from you."

"Wouldn't he have been able to tell pretty quickly that it was phony?"

"Of course. That's why so much depended on timing. They calculated that they would have a few hours' grace from the time he'd taken care of you until he discovered the fraud, hours in which they would be able to fly, without intervention, to Europe. They knew all too well that if he did not think he had the necklace himself, they wouldn't be permitted, any of them, to get through customs. They were all watched and they knew it. Their main chance, for now at least, was to throw him off the track long enough to make a getaway."

"And I was to be the one who ended up full of holes."

"That's about it. They assumed he would kill you or at least lock you up under some pretext or other until he had himself disposed of the jewels. It was perfectly sound reasoning. Mohammed Ali was taken in. You were taken in. It would have worked, too, if you hadn't come back a day early, shaking the Inspector in the process. Hélène had made plans to leave Cairo on the morning plane. Now, of course, she doesn't dare. Mohammed Ali would have her searched, will have anyone searched who might possibly be in league with her, and believe me, stupid as he is in many ways, he is perhaps the best-informed man in Egypt on smuggling. He has to be; he has made his fortune in commissions from smugglers. He knows every agent Said is apt to use, and more."

"Then Hélène has got the real necklace?"

"She was to leave the country as soon as she knew that you were in the hands of Mohammed Ali."

Pete whistled. He had not trusted her, but he'd never suspected her of a double-cross quite so dirty. It was an unpleasant feeling, to be expendable. "Has she gone yet?"

Le Mouche shook his head. "All this has made a difference," he said. "Not only your escape from the Inspector, but now the uprising. The airports are shut down. No one can leave the city, even by car. The roads are barricaded and there is nothing left for any of us to do, except wait. It is out of our hands. Allah has willed it."

Chapter Seven

But it was soon obvious to Pete that Allah was not the only one who had willed the disturbances. From bulletins that Le Mouche received by telephone every five or ten minutes, they learned that the fighting had been temporarily contained in the working-class suburbs of the city. With each message Pete became increasingly aware that Le Mouche, in some strange way, was one of the organizers of this rebellion, one of its generals. Yet no one came to the room. Only the telephone was continually busy; and it was not an ordinary telephone, Pete had discovered, but a radiophone.

He grew restless after a time. The noise of far-off gunfire excited him. It was the first he'd heard since France in the war. Finally he said, "I want to go out and look around. I ought to get my things at the hotel."

"I wouldn't advise that," said Le Mouche. "Mohammed Ali is still alive."

"Do you think he'll bother me when he knows I haven't got the necklace?"

"You are assuming that he is not vindictive, which is always a mistake. Keep away from your hotel. Forget the clothes."

"Maybe you're right. Maybe I should go to the Consulate and see if *they* know what's happening."

"An excellent idea. Stay there until tomorrow, until all this

is over. Then come back here and I will, I hope, have Anna
for you."

"If she's alive and if you're still here."

"And if heaven has not fallen down and broken your hard
head." Le Mouche smiled. "You must have a small amount of
optimism, Peter, to live at all. That may seem foolish advice
after what has happened, but…" The radiophone on the
table buzzed. Le Mouche picked up the receiver and spoke
into it.

Pete watched as the hunchback visibly paled. He spoke
Arabic rapidly, a scowl on his face, his tongue wetting his
lips nervously. Then he put the receiver down.

"Bad news?"

Le Mouche did not answer for a moment. He stared emptily into space. Then he nodded slowly, fixing his eyes on
Pete. "Bad for us but good for you."

"What do you mean? Has Anna—"

"Failed."

"Where is she?"

"Quite safe." Le Mouche sighed. "It was too much to expect.
She had only a slim chance, but even so, had she succeeded…
"

"Succeeded in what?"

"Regicide, I believe, is the word. It means king-killing. She
was to have murdered Farouk today. Unfortunately, before
she could see him, the trouble began in the city and he can-
celed all appointments. She was not able to carry out our
plan."

"Good Lord!" Pete was stunned.

"All this had been planned some months ago, shortly after I met her, quite by chance at the house of a mutual friend."

"You must've been crazy. There wasn't a chance in the world of her getting away with it. I may not know much about this town, but I did see that guy at a night club and he's as well guarded as any mobster back home."

Le Mouche shrugged. "The choice was as much hers as ours. She is as much involved as the rest of us—more so, in a strange way." Le Mouche paused; then: "I don't know how much you know about her past, but I expect she told you about her childhood among the Nazis, about her father and Dachau and all that. Well, these early experiences had a profound effect upon her. As a result, although ordinarily she is a charming girl, when it comes to tyrants she is a fanatic, and a little terrifying."

Pete shook his head, still bewildered. "I can't believe it."

"The complications began after she met you. A few months ago, when we decided upon this desperate course, she was bitter and hated the world, not caring if she lived or died. *I* cared, of course. I didn't want to see her sacrificed, but the choice was finally hers, not mine."

"Do you think anyone knows what she intended to do? The police, I mean?"

Le Mouche shook his head. "Only she and I knew, until this moment. The rest knew nothing more than that an attempt would be made upon the King's life—an assassination that would coincide with the first rioting in the El Minzah quarter of the city."

"Is she all right now? Was that her you talked to?"

"She is all right. That was one of our people out at Mena House. Several men were to break into the King's guesthouse nearby and rescue her if possible. When he did not arrive for the rendezvous, she went on to Shepheard's, where she will be safe for a little while."

"Safe? I thought you said—"

"Safe from the mob. I don't mean to alarm you, but there is a chance that our people, certain fanatics among them, may try to destroy the hotel."

"I've got to go there now," said Pete abruptly.

"In a few minutes, as soon as I get a report." He gestured toward the phone. "I should learn in a few minutes what is happening in that section of the city."

Pete sat back in his chair. Waiting was intolerable. He was tempted to leave anyway, on his own. But Le Mouche, as if guessing what he was thinking, shook his head. "You must wait. I insist on that."

"What's the best way to get her out of the city?"

"I think she will be able to answer that. It is quite true that she didn't expect to survive the assassination. Even though we had a group of men ready to rescue her at the cottage, there was not much chance they would get through the guards before the guards had killed her. Even so, because of you, she made plans for an escape—one that I was to tell you about at the proper time."

"The plans?"

"She must tell you now, since, for all I know, they've been

changed. But you can count on us to help you. I'll give you a safe-conduct through our lines. You will have to handle the government people yourself, but that shouldn't be too difficult, since they know nothing of Anna."

Pete grinned. "But they might just happen to be looking for me on account of Mohammed Ali."

Le Mouche frowned. "That is a problem."

"Well, just as long as I've got her with me, there won't be any trouble getting out of town. These people don't scare me one bit—in the daylight, anyway."

"Which reminds me I have an apology to make. The manager at the hotel in Luxor is one of our men. When he saw that Anna was becoming interested in you, he saw fit to arrange that business in the tombs."

Pete was surprised. The manager had been the last person he'd suspected. "But what was the big idea?"

"Anna was being watched by the police. It would have wrecked all our plans if the King had discovered she was involved with someone else. The manager acted quickly, ruthlessly, and without consulting any of us here. I was furious when I heard, but actually, he had only done his duty. Anna's interest in you might have ruined the whole affair."

"The old fellow, Osman—was he involved, too?"

"He was bribed to lead you into the tombs. He was killed that same night, to keep him from talking."

Pete whistled. "You fellows play rough."

"Very rough," said Le Mouche without a smile. "You were lucky and resourceful. Otherwise you would never have survived."

The radiophone buzzed and Le Mouche answered it. He asked a series of curt questions, nodding as the answers were given him. When he hung up, he turned to Pete. "You will have a difficult time getting through. There is a barricade in the streets between here and Shepheard's." He scribbled a few lines in Arabic on a sheet of paper, which he then folded and handed to Pete. "This should get you through our people —at least past the officers who can read. Pray that you don't get in the hands of the others. As for the police, the govern-ment people, you should have nothing to fear. Say you are an American trying to get to the hotel for safety."

"And Anna's there right now? Waiting for me?"

"She's there now. You have your gun? Good. Keep to the back streets. I hope your sense of direction is good, for they are like a maze. Go quickly. The hotel is in danger." Both men rose.

"Tell me," said Pete, "what's your connection with all this? Are you the boss of the show? Some kind of politician or something?"

The hunchback laughed. "Do I look like a boss? Or even a politician? Not likely. You might say that I am an adventurer corrupted by idealism. Now, my son, good-by. Allah be with you. We are not likely to meet again." They shook hands warmly, without further words; then Pete left Le Mouche alone in the small room with its radiophone and the two eye-holes that surveyed the crowded bar.

The back door was guarded by a half-dozen men with car-bines. They watched Pete closely but did not interfere when he moved down the narrow street to the main boulevard.

The boulevard was empty of ordinary traffic. The setting sun was dull gold upon the higher windows, casting dense purple shadows against the buildings with their shuttered doors. Far away in the northwest, he could hear artillery.

He stopped under the nearest arcade just as a jeep containing government soldiers clattered by. In the next few minutes several more trucks and jeeps moved rapidly down the boulevard, all going toward Shepheard's, away from the northwest and the firing.

Keeping close to the walls of buildings, he managed to walk the length of the block unnoticed. At the intersection he paused. Here trouble began.

A building several blocks away to the left was on fire, but no one attempted to put out the flames. A barricade had been thrown across the boulevard at this point and the police cars avoided it by driving to left and right, keeping at least two blocks distant of the mob that guarded the barricade: a haphazard collection of furniture, barrels, the body of a dead ox; a crazy fortification manned by an evil-looking assortment of men, wearing the long striped tunics of the fellahin, the workers. They were dangerously quiet, moving behind their cover, each carrying a rifle.

What to do next was a problem. The mob was in an ugly mood and Pete had already been warned that they would shoot on sight any man wearing European clothes, no matter what his nationality. Yet he had to get past that barricade, past at least a hundred trigger-happy Egyptians.

At first he thought of trying to explain to one of them that he was friendly, that he had a safe conduct from Le Mouche. But the risk involved was too great. They were apt to shoot on sight. The language barrier was also great.

He retreated deeper into the arcade. There was now no sign of life anywhere. No police, no citizens; even the million cats of Cairo had fled. The emptiness was reassuring.

An alleyway opening off the arcade provided him with a plan. He knew that the wide handsome avenues of Cairo had been arbitrarily cut through an ancient city of narrow crooked streets, a rabbit warren that still existed behind the great thoroughfares, a kind of Casbah where the secret Arab life went on. There were many entrances to this world, alleyways like the one before which he now stood. The only danger was that in the maze of crooked streets a stranger was easily lost, easily robbed, and as easily murdered.

He would have to take that chance. Gun in hand, he walked down the narrow alley. Knowing his position in relation to Le Couteau Rouge, he was able to guess at direction. His only danger was overshooting his mark, bypassing Shepheard's without knowing it.

The alley soon became a street just wide enough for three men to walk abreast. The pavement buckled crazily and there was a deep channel in the middle where, during the rains, the accumulated filth was carried off.

The odors were overpowering and he found it difficult to breathe. The evening was warm and all currents of fresh air were blocked by the several-story zigzag houses, whose wooden balconies touched overhead, hiding the sky.

Every few yards more streets branched off the one he was on, offering a bewildering number of alternatives, but he kept on course by checking the stars, which had begun to appear in the violet sky.

The people were abroad in these narrow streets. They obviously felt safe in their own territory. Yellow lamplight flickered in the windows. Occasionally he would pass an open door of a tea house, where he could see the natives sitting about on the floor drinking tea and talking in low guttural voices.

Those he met in the streets seemed more afraid of him than he was of them, stepping back against the walls to let him pass. None appeared to be armed. They gave the impression of people waiting for some great event. They were very quiet; there was none of the usual shouting and laughter that ordinarily characterized their section.

They were all listening to the gunfire, watching the red haze in the narrow strip of sky visible from the street. Their watchfulness made Pete nervous. They were like caged animals awaiting some signal, a sudden freedom. He walked more quickly, gun in hand; he was taking no chances. As he walked he kept a sharp lookout for possible attackers. But no one followed him or threatened him from the dark doorways. For once they were all too concerned with the common danger to prey upon strangers.

There was no trouble until he came to a small square.

The square was an irregular area twenty yards across with

a dozen streets like black holes in the shabby house fronts.
As he stood watching, from several of these streets men
came running in close pursuit of four soldiers that they had
flushed out of a building. Several of the attackers carried
torches. They were dangerously quiet as they circled the soldiers in the center of the square. Pete edged back into the
shadows and watched, horrified, as the soldiers threw down
their rifles and began to plead with the mob, which now had
swollen to nearly a hundred swarthy silent men. Then the
ringleader, a small man with eyes that glowed fiercely black
in the torchlight, approached one of the soldiers stealthily,
like a boxer coming out of his corner. Light gleamed on the
knife in his hand. The soldiers sank to their knees whim-
pering. Pete looked away, hearing the first terrible scream in
his head a good minute before it actually broke upon the
tense still air. It was like a signal. The mob began to shout
and curse, releasing its pent-up fury in a chaos of sound.

Pete pressed into a doorway, thankful for its depth. Men
came running down the street past him. Fortunately, none
saw him. There were three more hoarse screams clearly
audible above the mob's roar; then the sound of many feet
running and the light of torches grew dim as the mob moved
on to another part of the quarter.

He waited until there was neither light nor sound; then
he looked out into the square. It was deserted except for four
huddled shapes. He tried not to look at them as he walked
quickly across the courtyard, but one brief glimpse showed
they had been beheaded.

He plunged once more into the maze of streets, all deserted now. Not even lamplight shone in the narrow windows. The wooden balconies were empty. The passage of the mob had frightened even its own kind, and the people hid behind shutters in darkened rooms.

Then, just as he was positive that he was hopelessly lost, a turn of a crooked street, so narrow that at points he could touch opposing walls, brought him onto a modern thorough-fare. He had arrived at last.

Shepheard's had a dozen soldiers in front, guarding this headquarters of European and American interests. He was let through without any delay by a sergeant who satisfied himself with one hard look that he belonged there.

The lobby was crowded with worried-looking men and women. Many of them had suitcases piled about them, belongings that they had brought from other, less safe, hotels and from their homes. These were residents of the city, come here for safety.

Pete crossed the front lobby looking for Anna. He had got as far as the bar when he bumped into Hastings.

"God's sake! *There* you are. Looking all over Cairo for you. Afraid something happened to you. Get a drink, eh? If we can." Hastings led Pete into the bar and they sat at the one empty table in the room and ordered gin. The room was packed with British and Americans talking in low, tight voices about "the situation."

"Heard some strange rumors about you, boy. Seems there was trouble at your hotel. Manager didn't know what, when we asked. Said something about your leaving, and then said they d found Mohammed Ali in your room, looking green around the gills. What happened?" Hastings gave a good performance of an interested and sympathetic friend.

"Just about what you'd expect," said Pete, playing along. "He came up there to get the necklace. We had a fight and—"

"He didn't get it?" There was no mistaking the urgency of this.

"No, he didn't get it." Hastings sighed with relief. "But I thought I'd better get out of there and make myself invisible, for a while."

"Smart boy. Then you still have it?"

Pete nodded. "I'm not letting it go without a fight," he said. "I don't think the Inspector will bother me for it again."

"I wouldn't be too sure of that. He's tipped his hand. He's shown us, Said especially, that he's after it, in spite of agreements, commissions, and so on. Said will get him. Never fear Said will have his head, but meanwhile Mohammed Ali is a clever chap. He can't afford to give up now. He's done for in Egypt. His only hope is to get the article in question away from you and slip over the border."

"You haven't seen him, have you?" asked Pete.

"Who? The Inspector? Not a sign. Doubt if he'll be around, either. Of course, all this mess changes everything." And Hastings swore irritably for a moment.

"Just what is it, the mess? What's going on?"

Hastings shrugged. "Don't know any more than what I read in the papers. Papers say Jews. God knows *what* they mean. Lot of trouble between the Grand Mufti and the

Zionists. Maybe the Mufti's getting back at them. Probably all a fake, staged by the government so they can lock up a few malcontents. Good plan, too. Suggest it for other countries. Always a lot of sour apples in every country complaining. Fine. Let them complain. Then one day—boom! Say *they* started it. Lock 'em up. Do away with the lot. Only way to keep order."

"But think how it hurts their feelings," said Pete mockingly.

"Have no sympathy for them. Hitler was a bad egg, but by God, he had the right idea about running things."

"I expect you're right," said Pete, disguising his contempt. Hastings represented the last word in the Neanderthal mind. "Does the government have everything under control?"

"Looks like it, but then riots never happen around here, never around Shepheard's. Natives scared to death of it. Seat of the British lion and all that. They'd never touch the hotel. That's why people flock here instead of to the consulates and embassies."

"Maybe all this will give Mohammed Ali something else to think about."

Hastings nodded. "I'm sure he's under orders. Probably won't see him until the trouble's blown over."

"So isn't this the best time to get the necklace out of the country?"

Hastings chuckled grimly. "Try and get across the river even. Try to get a taxi. It's impossible. We're all trapped."

"Have you checked on planes?" This was malicious, but Pete played it straight.

"Planes? No. That is, we know what everyone knows.

Government in charge of airports. No flights out."

"And said? Wasn't he supposed to give us the word today? Wasn't this to be the day we make a break for it?"

"Not sure," said Hastings evasively. "No word from him. Don't know how much he knows about conditions here. Blackout on radios."

"You think the government'll survive?"

"Certainly. Fat Boy may be objectionable in ways, but he's tough; he'll hold on."

Pete drank his gin; he felt better, less shaky. "What do you think I ought to do now?"

"Hang around here, I'd say. Don't want you out in the streets with all that loot. Snipers in the area, or so they say."

"Is Hélène here?"

"Yes. Want to give her a call?"

"Think I might. See you." And Pete left the Englishman in the bar; but instead of going to Hélène's room he searched the now crowded lobbies. Anna was nowhere in sight and he was growing uneasy.

In the front lobby he paused among the murmuring, frightened Europeans, all listening to the firing, which had perceptibly increased. A little of the combined terror in the lobby rubbed off on him, terror for Anna, not for himself.

Finally he asked the desk clerk if he had seen Anna Mueller, and to his surprise and relief the harassed man nodded. "She's here somewhere." But that was all he knew. Pete continued his search.

Convinced at last that she was not in any of the lobbies or in the garden, he walked aimlessly down corridors. There was a chance she had gone to the room of some friend. Unintentionally, he found himself at Hélène's door. On an impulse, he knocked.

"Come in." She was seated at her writing table when he entered. She was alone. Pete hesitated for a split second; then he slipped the bolt in the door behind him. This was as good a time as any to finish the business.

If she was frightened or startled, she did not show it. Smiling, she rose. "I have been waiting all day to hear from you. Come, sit down." They sat opposite one another. "I was terribly worried, Peter. Especially after the rioting started in the city."

"I had a little visit from Mohammed Ali."

"So we heard. It must've been terrible." She lit a cigarette with a steady hand. He admired her coolness. "You must stay here until the emergency, as they are calling it, is over."

"I plan to."

"What happened with Mohammed Ali?"

"He wanted the necklace, like everybody else. He didn't get it, but we had a good fight."

"Thank God!" Her performance, he noted, was faultless. "We were insane to let you go back to the Stanley. He would never have dared do anything like that here."

"How did you know what happened at the Stanley?"

"Hastings told me. He found out. We didn't know whether or not Mohammed Ali had got the necklace, though. We were told only about the fight."

"What would you have done if he had got it?"

She shuddered. "Don't even suggest it!"

"I wouldn't. Not for the world," he mocked.

She could not ignore his tone this time. "What is wrong, *chéri*? Has anything happened?"

He chuckled. "Only a fight with the law and a revolution. Nothing serious."

"Soon it will all be like a bad dream," she said soothingly. "It's not easy for any of us, but then you were warned that there'd be trouble, that you were taking a risk."

"I didn't realize what kind of risk it was until today."

She pretended not to understand. "In a day or two you'll be able to leave Egypt, for good, if you like, with the necklace. Said has great faith in you. He told me fine things about you."

"I'm sure he did. After all, I was exactly what he was looking for."

"We needed a stranger, unknown in Egypt, and unafraid of people like Mohammed Ali. You were just right."

"Even better, maybe." There was a loud crash of artillery. A windowpane shattered. The guns were coming closer. Above the garden, Pete saw planes in the evening sky.

"I hate all that," said Hélène, looking out the window at the planes. "It was like this when Rommel was outside the city."

"And you and Erich Raedermann were inside."

"That is no concern of yours," she said sharply, turning back to him.

"I guess not. But we were talking about me, about how good I was for this job."

She smiled. "You are very vain. Yes, you've been good, better than even I had hoped, and remember, it was I who chose you."

"I won't forget."

The grimness was unmistakable now; she could no longer pretend not to understand. "What are you trying to say?"

"Only that there isn't too much time and we ought to get things straight."

"But everything *is* straight. You must wait here until we can get a plane for you. Said will be able to fix something. I'm sure of that."

"So I'll hang around here until Mohammed Ali shows up and does a real job on me, which will then be your cue to float off into the wild blue yonder."

She looked puzzled "I…I don't understand you."

"I threw it away. Maybe you understand that."

"Threw it away? Threw *what* away?"

"The bit of Woolworth junk you wanted me and Mohammed Ali to believe was the real thing, the real necklace that you planned to skip town with today."

She was very white now. "You're insane! You couldn't have destroyed it. That was the real necklace."

For a moment he was shaken. But he remembered that she was a good actress and he did not waver. They were both on their feet now. He walked toward her. She backed away until the wall stopped her. Her eyes were wide and glowing with strange emotions.

"No, it wasn't real. I know. I had it looked at by someone who did know, and then, after I was sure it was fake, I knew what the game was, what you all had planned for me." He was standing over her now, and he looked down at her and said quietly, "I want the real one."

"I don't know what you're talking about," she whispered. She tried to move away. He stopped her, aware of that faint jasmine odor he had noticed the first time they met, and the second. He would pay her back for the second.

"I've been on to you a long time now," he said. "I was suspicious from the first. It was too phony, sending me up there without knowing me at all, except for your little investigation on the side. It was especially phony when I saw that everybody in the damned country seemed to know what I was up to, particularly the one joker who shouldn't have known anything, the Inspector. From the first day he came around to my room and told me he was interested in our caper, I figured that I was being used in some way that wasn't clear."

"But you knew that he was part of this, that he always got payment whenever we sent anything abroad." She spoke quickly, nervously.

"No, I was supposed to be the fall guy. Well, it almost worked. Mohammed Ali almost took care of me today. He may still, though I doubt it. I don't intend to hang around here until he comes, as you'd like me to. The second the roads are free, I'm gone. I've had it."

"Said will kill you." Her voice was cold and hard.

"Let him try. He'll have to find me first."

"He will. He has friends in every country. You'll never escape."

"I'll take my chances. I expect he's going to be too busy with local problems to worry about me, though I guess he's going to be pretty mad, especially now."

"After your destroying the necklace?" Her performance was wearing thin.

"Worse than that." Peter grinned at her. "I'm taking it. I want the original."

She gasped and tried to break away. He held her against the wall. "You're out of your mind! There is no other."

"I want it. Give it to me."

She started to scream but he was too quick for her. He clapped his hand over her mouth. "You've got it. I know you have. Get it for me or I'll—"

Her answer was to bite his hand. With a curse he jumped back and she made a break for the door. Before she could unbolt it, though, he caught her again. He held her by her long black hair. She did not scream as he led her back into the room. Her eyes flashed with rage.

"I haven't got much time," he said, looking down into her face. "I expect our friend Hastings will be along any minute to find out what's happened to us. So give me that necklace."

"There isn't any other. I swear—" She gasped as he suddenly twisted her hair. Then: "I—I don't have it. Said's got it, in Luxor." He was triumphant; at last the story was confirmed.

"I'm going to count to ten," he said quietly. "If you don't give it to me then, I'll break your neck, like this." And he pulled her head back sharply.

"Peter, I don't have it. I swear I don't!"

"One."

"I'd give it to you, *chéri,* believe me I would, but—"

"Two."

"Said is bringing it tomorrow from Luxor. He was supposed to come today but—"

"Three."

"Wait until then. I'll give it to you, *chéri.* Come to the hotel
tomorrow and I promise—"

"Four."

"We can leave together. You were interested in me, weren't
you? A little? I was in you, you know that. You could tell. I hate
Said. I always have, but I was poor and he promised me—"

"Five."

"He forced me to love him, to work for him. To send you to
Luxor. I know I was weak. I didn't want anything to happen to
you, believe me, but those were his orders, his and Hastings'.
I couldn't—"

"Six."

"I'd planned to tell you, to let you know before it was too
late. I hoped all along that Mohammed Ali wouldn't attack. I
thought it was enough that he suspected you had it. That was
all. And that he'd only try to—"

"Seven."

She was speaking rapidly now, her breath coming in quick
gasps and her face as pale as ice. "Peter, it still isn't too late.
We can leave Egypt together. I'll work for you. I have friends
in Europe, in Paris. They'll take care of us. You'll be rich. We
can live together."

"Eight."

"We'll take the necklace from Said. We'll sell it in Paris. We can live almost a lifetime there on the money from it."

"Nine."

"Peter *chéri,* please *listen* to me!" The scarlet mouth drew closer to his own. The warm body pressed against his. Waves of desire threatened to engulf him. He faltered. And she, conscious that he was aroused, spoke more slowly, more lovingly, caressing him with her hands, her voice, as the scarlet mouth moved closer to his own.

With a tremendous effort of will, like the snapping of chains, he shook his head and almost shouted: "Ten!"

The next moment was one of confusion. She brought her knee up sharply between his legs. He let go of her, doubling up with pain. She broke away, got to her dressing table, and drew out a revolver. By the time he had recovered, she was in charge of the situation. She stood in the center of the room, the pistol aimed at his chest, the old mocking smile on her lips. Her hair, loosened by his grip, flowed like a dark waterfall about her shoulders.

"What a fool you are, Peter! But not foolish enough, perhaps, for now you must be killed."

"Go ahead." Pete had got his wind back; he was able to straighten up, the sharp pain succeeded by an ache.

"But at least it would have been better to die ignorant at Mohammed Ali's hands." She laughed. "Now it will be worse. Especially since you think you're in love with that German tramp. Oh, I've heard. Not that it prevented you from feeling just a little *excité* with me." She laughed contemptuously.

He saw her through a darkening rage that made even the lights of the room grow dim. All he could see was that mocking vivid mouth. But he controlled himself and spoke quietly. "I guess nothing worked out right " he said. "Even us."

"No, not even us." She smiled. "I had always looked forward to it, *chéri*. One of those things that I thought might be enjoyable."

"Maybe it's not too late for that."

She looked at him curiously. "You could still…after all this? And after her?"

He nodded. "You saw a minute ago; you could tell."

She shook her head. "I'm not so easily tricked."

"You've got the gun. What are you afraid of?"

"No one can make love with a gun," she said, but she moved closer to him. "It is a pity such a handsome animal must die," she murmured.

It happened easily. One swift blow of his left fist aimed at the mouth and she fell to the floor without a sound. He kicked the gun from her nerveless fingers. Then the lights went out and the hotel rocked, as a thunderous noise sounded outside in the street. A bomb had gone off and all the windows were shattered. The sudden darkness was pierced by screams and shouts.

He lit his cigarette lighter and made a feverish search of the room. There was no necklace. He wondered if she had been telling the truth, if Said still had it. He kept an eye on her but she was unconscious, her face covered by her heavy silken hair. In the dressing table he found the jewel box from which she had taken the money to pay him. This would do, he thought grimly, and he stuck it in his pocket. Then he left the room and walked quickly down the hall.

The lobby was a nightmare of screaming women and shouting men. In the street outside a sharp crack of rifles told him that the mob had got through at last. Shepheard's was being attacked.

He had to find Anna. Seizing a torch from a frightened servant, he pushed his way through the milling crowd.

The refugees had moved from the front lobby to the center one and to the bar at the back of the hotel, away from the street and the guns.

Hands clutched at him, as though for support. Men shoved him as they tried to get from the main lobby to the comparative safety of the bar. Bullets raked the front of the hotel. A woman crumpled to the floor beside him, whether dead or only fainted he had no time to find out. He found Anna standing in an alcove near the bar. The light of his torch illuminated her face suddenly, briefly. He fought his way through a tangle of people to the alcove where she stood.

"Peter!" She fell into his arms and for a brief moment they stood there in the center of a panic, aware only of one another, but the crash of a grenade outside in the street brought him back to reality, to a frightening reality. "Where were you? I looked all over." They stepped into the alcove as a group of sweating, wild-eyed soldiers fell back into the central lobby and took up a tentative position, their rifles pointed at the main door.

"Telephoning. The German boy, the flier who brought us from Luxor. He's waiting for us, Peter. Right now, at Giza."

"He's going to—"

"Fly us to Naples, yes. But we have only two hours to get

there, to get outside Cairo."

"Come on, then." Hugging the wall, they moved toward the bar, where Pete remembered a door led into the garden. There was just a chance that the garden was not surrounded. If so, they could climb the iron fence and slip into a side street.

Before they had got to the door, however, an explosion that shook the building to its foundations threw them sprawling onto the floor. There was a sudden ghastly silence, then moans and cries of pain as a sheet of flame swirled up the walls of the front lobby, casting a lurid glow over everything, like a scene in hell. The hotel was on fire.

"Are you all right?"

Anna nodded, getting to her feet dizzily, holding her head. "Yes, I think so."

"Come on. Before this place blows up."

Others now had the same idea he had had. They were swarming into the garden, climbing the tall iron fence, their figures curiously distorted by the flaring light of the now flaming hotel.

Halfway across the garden, they encountered Hastings. He looked as cool, as hard as ever, in spite of the revolver he held in his hand. "Hand it over, Wells." For a second they faced one another in the ruddy light.

"Hand what over?"

There was a perceptible click, a small sound but ominous, audible beneath the shouts and noise of firing in the street. Hastings aimed carefully at Pete's heart. Anna, who had been standing nearest Hastings, threw herself upon him like a lioness, pushing his arm up. The pistol went off into the air. Hastings reeled under the attack. Before he could take aim again, Pete was upon him.

With the hilt of his own revolver, he clubbed the Englishman into unconsciousness. Then he seized Anna by the arm and together they ran toward the garden's gate and into the street.

They ran several blocks without stopping; then, suddenly, both exhausted, they stopped and leaned against the shuttered window of a shop until they had got their breath.

Pete looked about them at the darkened street. No street lamps were on and the starlight was dim. A murky red haze in the sky to the west marked the flaming ruins of Shepheard's Hotel.

"Where do you think we are?"

Anna shook her head. "I'm not sure. I don't know this quarter. But we must find some way to get across the Nile."

"How far is Giza?"

"Several miles from Mena House, on the other side." She pushed her tangled hair back from her face; a smear of soot darkened her pale forehead. Pete was aware that his own clothes were torn and smelled of smoke and gunpowder. The jewel box was still in his pocket.

"Our only stunt is to get a car. Would you know the way if I drove?"

"I think so, yes. But we don't have—"

"We'll find one. I used to be kind of good at that sort of thing." They moved cautiously back toward the firing, circling the hotel, keeping to arcades and dark side streets.

They did not see one human being until they had got onto
the main boulevard, which crossed the street on which
Shepheard's had been. Here they found themselves in the
center of the government forces. Jeeps with searchlights
patrolled the streets. Convoy trucks rushed soldiers to a barricade, which they could just make out at the end of the
wide boulevard, but the firing that had been so noticeable
earlier was growing more sporadic, fainter.

In front of a shattered store front, they stopped; a column
shielded them from the searchlights raking the streets. Two
dead men were sprawled before the store, as though caught
in the act of looting. Across the street a single jeep was
parked, and beside it a group of uniformed men were talking
excitedly. Farther down the street more jeeps had gathered
and there was occasional firing; it sounded to Pete as if snipers
were being picked off.

"You drive?" he whispered. She nodded. In a low tense
voice he explained to her what he would try to do. It was
dangerous, but if she was frightened she did not show it.

They separated then. She moved down the arcade to the
opposite corner while he crossed the street a half block
above the point where the jeep was parked. The searchlight
was trained on the second floor of a building across the
street, leaving enough darkness to cover him. The men by
the jeep, four of them, were still arguing.

He waited until he was sure Anna was within a few yards
of the jeep; then he opened fire on the men, aiming just
above their heads. His first bullet ricocheted with a whine
into the street. The men, startled, fell back against the wall

and returned the fire with their carbines. Pete retreated. They followed, creeping with bellies against the walls of buildings, pausing in occasional doorways to fire. When he had got them a dozen yards from their jeep, he made a break for it.

He ran the remaining few feet of the arcade with the chilling noise of bullets around him, like deadly bees. Then he ducked into the side street that he had noticed from the other side. Praying that it would double around the way he had calculated, he ran with all possible speed down the dark tunnel-like street, stumbling over the uneven pavement. He was closely pursued; they had taken the bait. He was thankful for the darkness of the night and the narrowness of the street. No starlight lessened the gloom; visibility did not extend more than a few yards. He was invisible to his pursuers and they to him except when the red flash of a carbine shattered the darkness behind him.

The break in the street came at about the point he had expected, a block and a half below the place where the jeep had been parked. Panting, his shirt clammy with sweat and his lungs burning, he ran into the boulevard just as Anna passed him in the jeep. He shouted to her, a noise more like an animal's than a man's.

She stopped and began to back up. With two long strides and a jump he was in the seat beside her. She was shifting gears with a screech as the soldiers came out onto the boulevard. One opened fire but his aim was wild and the jeep had turned the corner on two wheels before the others had got the range.

They traded positions and Pete drove according to her

directions.

They kept to deserted streets as much as possible, moving toward the river, away from the fighting and the burning hotel.

They encountered no police until they came to the bridge that crossed the Nile. As Pete had feared, a dozen men held the bridge, checking all traffic.

He made a lightning decision. His only alternatives were both risky: either to stop and bluff his way across or to drive straight through the cordon of men. He stopped.

"Who's in charge here?" he shouted in a loud bullying voice. The two policemen who were closing in on the jeep fell back, confused, not understanding English but recognizing the tone of authority.

"I am in charge, sir," said a voice in English, and out of the shadows stepped Mohammed Ali. He was as startled as Pete. Inadvertently he shied back when he saw the American, his hand leaping to his holster.

"I'm taking Miss Mueller to Mena House, where she'll be safe. They've set fire to Shepheard's." Pete knew his bluff was doomed from the start.

"I'll be happy to escort her, Mr. Wells," said Mohammed Ali and he turned to Anna. "Please get down." The moment the Inspector turned his glance away from him, Pete shifted into first, his foot pressed hard on the clutch. Before Mohammed Ali had time to notice what he had done, Pete said, "They gave us this jeep at Shepheard's. I have an authorization." Mohammed Ali looked startled; the revolver he had had trained on Pete wavered. "Where is your driver, then?"

"They weren't able to give us one. Too much going on. I was told to take her across the river." Pete spoke quickly.

"I should be very interested in seeing the authorization," said the Inspector. He grinned slyly as he released the safety catch on his revolver.

"I've got it right here," said Pete, reaching into his coat. Then, in one instant, synchronizing his foot on the clutch with his hand on his pistol, he fired through his coat at the Inspector and drove the jeep straight through the line of policemen, who ran, yelling, for cover. Mohammed Ali spun and fell face downward on the bridge. The jeep was halfway across the bridge when the police started firing.

Pete shoved Anna to the floor; then, crouched over the wheel, expecting death at any minute, he drove at top speed across the bridge and onto the main highway beyond. A sharp retort told him that one of his rear tires had been shot. But he drove on, the tire flapping against the pavement until only the metal rim was left.

Luckily, there was neither fighting nor police on this side of the river. The streets were empty in the gray dawn. The police on the bridge did not follow. They drove on into the desert toward Giza.

A few miles beyond the last suburb, they saw the plane parked on the side of the road. "Thank God, he's still there," murmured Anna.

The pilot was relieved too. "I thought it was bad news," he said as he helped Anna out of the jeep. "We start now, before daylight."

While he revved up the engines, Pete and Anna got into the plane. Anna immediately took up the earphones and switched on the radio while Pete pulled out the jewel box and pried it open with his pocket knife.

There, among the diamonds and sapphires of Hélène de Rastignac, was the necklace of Queen Tiy, intricate and magnificent, its single ruby gleaming like firelight. Anna saw it, too, her attention diverted from the radio, her eyes wide with wonder.

"What is this?" she asked.

Pete told her, told her how much it was worth and what it would mean to them. She touched it curiously. "And the rest of these things?"

"A present to me from Hélène."

"You stole them?"

"No. I took them in exchange for services rendered. I expect I got them as honestly as she did." And, as well as he could above the plane's roar, he told her about the conspiracy to get the necklace out of Egypt with himself as decoy and fall guy. But before he had finished, she had pushed the earphones back over her ears. He could tell by her face that the news was not good.

"Do you think they'll catch Le Mouche?" he asked when she had switched off the radio.

She shook her head. "No, he will disappear into the old quarter of the city, until the next time."

"You think there'll be a next time?"

"Oh, yes. The Farouks never last long, even in countries

like Egypt."

"A place we'll never see again."

She smiled at last. "Is it so wonderful, really, your country?"

"You'll see." The plane had now taxied into the wind and was taking off. The last stars of the night were burning out in the gray sky.

"I'm so tired," she murmured, and he took her in his arms.

"It's all over," he said soothingly, "it's all over." She fell asleep then, her head against his chest, unaware that a new white sun had risen, striking silver on the land before them.